CHAPTER ONE

He often wondered if we were all characters in one of God's dreams.

The first thing he discerned when he regained consciousness was a woman in white. This angel was calling him by his first name, Tom, although they had never been introduced.

'Are you a nun?' he said.

'No, I'm Jasmine. I'm a nurse. Come on, Tom, I've got to wake you up. I've got to put this other pillow under your head. And lift the top part of your bed. Like this . . .' She manipulated with her foot a lever of the hospital bed so that he was slightly raised. 'Otherwise,' she said, 'you might feel groggy.' She stuck a thermometer in his mouth before he had time to speak, and took his wrist in her hand, looking at her watch. He saw by her watch that it was twenty past twelve.

The sun was visible behind the curtains, so it must have been daytime.

He dozed off while she was still counting his pulse. When he woke half an hour later as it seemed, it was dark, it was ten-forty at night as he learned from the new nurse, the night nurse, name of Edna so she told him. So does our trade direct our perceptions and our dreams he thought: Tom was a film director. Cut into the scene of the morning with the scene of the evening. The same nurse, but was it the same? Anyway it was Edna and the same scene.

'Where's the doctor?' Tom said.

'He looked in this afternoon. Were you awake?'

'Perhaps.' Tom wasn't sure. He thought he might remember a doctor's face looming over him.

Edna let his bed down by manipulating the lever. There was a drip inserted in his foot that he had been aware of since he woke but hadn't been able to remark on. Edna was nearly black of skin. 'Where do you come from, Edna?' 'Ghana,' she said, or was he mixing her up with someone else? When he woke it was the daylight of early morning.

Enter a lady in white, this time with a head-veil. 'You are one of the nuns?' She was. She was Sister Felicitas come to take a sample of his blood.

'They took my blood already,' he said.

'That was your urine.'

'What are you going to do with my blood?'

'Drink it,' she said.

'What time is it?'

'Seven.'

'How can you be so larky so early in the morning?'

PENGUIN BOOKS

REALITY AND DREAMS

Muriel Spark was born and educated in Edinburgh, and has been active in the field of creative writing since 1950, when she won a short-story competition in the *Observer*. Her many subsequent novels and stories, such as *Memento Mori*, *The Girls of Slender Means*, *The Only Problem*, *A Far Cry From Kensington* and *The Prime of Miss Jean Brodie* (adapted successfully for both film and theatre), have brought pleasure to readers throughout the world. She has also written plays, poems, children's books and biographies of Mary Shelley, Emily Brontë and John Masefield. Her first autobiographical volume, *Curriculum Vitae*, was published in 1992. She was elected C.Litt. in 1992 and was awarded the DBE in 1993. Among many other awards she has received the Italia Prize, the James Tait Black Memorial Prize, the FNAC Prix Etranger, the Saltire Prize, the Ingersoll T. S. Eliot Award and the David Cohen British Literature Prize in recognition of a lifetime's literary achievement. Dame Muriel was elected an honorary member of the American Academy of Arts and Letters in 1978 and Commandeur de L'Ordre des Arts et des Lettres in France in 1996.

Reality and Dreams was winner of a Scottish Arts Council 1997 Spring Book Award.

BY MURIEL SPARK IN PENGUIN

Fiction

The Comforters
Robinson
Memento Mori
The Ballad of Peckham Rye
The Bachelors
The Prime of Miss Jean Brodie
The Girls of Slender Means
The Mandelbaum Gate
The Public Image
The Driver's Seat
Not to Disturb
The Hothouse by the East River
The Abbess of Crewe
The Takeover
Territorial Rights
Loitering with Intent
The Only Problem
A Far Cry from Kensington
Symposium
The Collected Stories of Muriel Spark
Reality and Dreams

Autobiography

Curriculum Vitae

Muriel Spark

REALITY
AND
DREAMS

PENGUIN BOOKS

PENGUIN BOOKS

Published by the Penguin Group
Penguin Books Ltd, 27 Wrights Lane, London W8 5TZ, England
Penguin Putnam Inc., 375 Hudson Street, New York, New York 10014, USA
Penguin Books Australia Ltd, Ringwood, Victoria, Australia
Penguin Books Canada Ltd, 10 Alcorn Avenue, Toronto, Ontario, Canada M4V 3B2
Penguin Books (NZ) Ltd, 182–190 Wairau Road, Auckland 10, New Zealand

Penguin Books Ltd, Registered Offices: Harmondsworth, Middlesex, England

First published by Constable and Company Ltd 1996
Published in Penguin Books 1997
1 3 5 7 9 10 8 6 4 2

Acknowledgement is made to
the estate of T. S. Eliot and to Faber & Faber
for permission to quote from
'The Love Song of J. Alfred Prufrock'

The moral right of the author has been asserted

Printed in England by Clays Ltd, St Ives plc

REALITY AND DREAMS

'It's late. We rise at five.'

'Was that you singing? I heard singing.'

'That was us in the chapel.'

She was gone in a whisk of white. In came his breakfast tray, supporting it seemed, dusky Edna.

'Do you call this breakfast?'

'First you get liquid, then soft, then solid.'

She poured out some milky tea. He opened his eyes. The tray had disappeared.

He was now thinking of the plans he had made, the vow he had taken, before his operation. He intended to keep it.

'Good morning.'

Two women came in with a mop and pail. One dusted while the other slopped the floor of that room in the international hospital. Now two nurses came to make his bed. They got him up. They helped him through to the bathroom. They shaved him with expert hands. Oh go on shaving, it's nice. But then they unplugged the razor. Someone had put an enormous bunch of flowers on the far table, a mixture of roses, lilies and asters, most remarkable and expensive.

The surgeon: You're going to be all right.

What did he mean, I'm going to be all right? So earnest. I never thought I wasn't.

Beside his bed a table on wheels, moveable to any convenient angle. On the table was a telephone. Good, I will wait till I feel a bit stronger, after the liquids and the soft.

'When will I be on solids, Edna?'

'I'm not Edna, I'm Greta. You have solids tomorrow.'

'Greta, where do you come from?'

'Hamburg.'

He felt like a casting director. Greta is absolutely built for the part. But which part?

The telephone rang.

The difficulty of his turning to lift the receiver was solved by Greta who wheeled the table to an angle where the phone was close to hand.

'Yes?' His voice croaked.

'Is that you, Tom? Tom, is that you?'

'I suppose so. I'll be on solids tomorrow.' He was actually wider awake than he wanted anyone to know.

'I suppose I can come and visit this afternoon?'

'No, tomorrow.'

Claire, Tom's wife, arrived in the afternoon. He hadn't yet told her the plans he had made. She would be intrigued by them but not anxious. That was one advantage of having a very rich wife. You could make plans without her worrying immediately how it was going to affect her budget. Tom once had a wife who referred back every action, every thought of his, to her budget. She was much happier divorced with a well-paid job of her own.

He had a belly-ache. Came Sister Benedict with her injection.

'Tom! ... Tom! ...'

Claire was by his bed, smiling, holding his hand. 'You're going to be all right,' she said.

Nobody had said he wasn't.

He said, 'I want to see Fortescue-Brown.' That was his lawyer, full of fuss and business, never letting you get a word in. I only keep him, thought Tom, because I am too genuinely busy to change.

'Fortescue-Brown!' said Claire.

'Yes, Fortescue-Brown,' he said.

'At a moment like this you want to see Fortescue-Brown?'

'That's right,' he said.

She pulled up a chair and sat close to his bed, pushing the wheeled table out of the way. When he looked again only the chair was there and a nurse was coming in with a tray of filthy supper.

'What is your name?'

'Ruth.'

'Well, Ruth, I can't eat that white soup.'

'What would you like to eat? I'll ask for something else.'

'I am straining every muscle in my imagination to think of something else. Forget it.'

'You have to keep your strength up,' said Ruth. She had a tiny waist and an enormous backside. He couldn't keep his eyes off it. She was about thirty with straw-coloured hair drawn back, and a pale face. She would have cast well as a German spy in those old days of yore. She disappeared and to his amazement came back with an egg *en cocotte* which he consumed absent-mindedly.

'Are you expecting any visitor this evening?' Ruth had come to take away the tray. By her watch it was half past six.

'My daughter, Marigold, an unfrocked priest of a woman.'

Marigold was suddenly there.

'Well, Pa, I hear you're going to be all right,' said she, with her turned-down smile, skinnily slithering into a chair and arranging her coat over her flat chest. She should never have married. No wonder her husband James had decided to write travel books.

'How's James?' Tom said.

'So far as I know he's in Polynesia.'

'I said how, not where.'

'Don't wear yourself out,' she said, 'with too much conversation. I bought you some grapes.' She said 'bought' not 'brought'. She dumped a plastic bag on the side table. 'This is a wonderful clinic,' she said. 'I suppose it costs a fortune. Of course nothing should be spared in a case like yours.'

You must not imagine Marigold was particularly deprived.

In the morning Tom rang Fortescue-Brown and made an appointment for him to come to the clinic at three in the afternoon.

Love and economics, Tom mused. 'I have always,' he thought, 'considered them as opposites. Why do they continually bump into each other as if they were allied topics? Is it possible that what I call love isn't love?'

He was touched that lovely Cora his daughter by his first wife had flown into London to see him. She had obtained leave for the occasion from whatever she was doing in Lyons for Channel Four. Her first words were 'Pa, you're going to be all right.' She went on to say how her husband, Johnny, had been declared redundant at his job, an administrator in Parsimmons & Gould the paint people. She continued that she had managed to get a cheap bucket-shop flight to see him. 'And what,' thought he, 'has Johnny's redundancy got to do with me, my broken ribs and thigh? And her cheap flight? Did she come for love or what?

'And I am glad,' he continued in his mind, 'that Johnny has been made redundant. I am glad with the gladness of the lover of truth: the man has always been superfluous.'

He said, 'Marigold has been here.'

'I know,' said Cora.

'She brought me some grapes,' Tom put in experimentally.

'I know,' said Cora. 'Don't you want to watch the news?'

There was a television in the corner, stuck up on the wall, and a controller by the side table. Tom switched it on. A Nigerian politician being interviewed – 'Democracy,' he said, 'is not a one-man cup of tea.' Tom switched off.

'Are you in pain?' said Fortescue-Brown.

'Yes, indeed, Mr. Brown, I am.'

'Now, Tom,' said he, 'reflect. You are getting angry again. Angry and arrogant. There was no need, no need at all, for you to go up on that crane. An ordinary dolly is perfectly all right for directing a motion picture these days. But no, you have to be different, you have to be right up there beside the photographer, squeezed in, and without a seat-belt. You have to be God.'

'Are you suggesting that God wears a seat-belt?'

'Nothing, nothing would surprise me after being your lawyer for twenty years. When do you get out of this penitentiary?'

'Next week, but I have to take two nurses home with me.'

'Two?'

'One for day and one for night. Is it your money or mine?'

'I told you to take out an insurance.'

'Well I didn't. Find some money. Scratch around.'

He was no sooner out of the door than Tom chucked a tumbler full of water at the door, so that Fortescue-Brown could hear it. Broken glass and water all over the place. There was something else he had wanted to say to the lawyer, but never mind. There was a vow. But what vow?

As the cleaners mopped it up Tom smiled sweetly at them. 'It just flew out of my hand as I sat up.'

'Don't try to sit up, Mr. Richards. Just ring the bell.'

Tom lay thinking . . . Yes, I did feel like God up on that crane. It was wonderful to shout orders through the amplifier and like God watch the team down there group and re-group as bidden. Especially those two top stars and the upstart minor stars, with far too much money, thinking they could direct the film better themselves. There was none of the 'Just a minute, may I suggest . . .' that held up my work constantly on the floor. Right up there I was beyond and above pausing a minute and listening to their suggestions. What do they think a film set is? A democracy, or something? I simply don't regret that crane for a moment. All I want to know is who fouled us up. Who made the wheels hiccup on the tangle of wires, so that I was thrown clean off, crash. Twelve ribs and a broken hip, and lucky, very lucky, to be alive.

CHAPTER TWO

As Tom Richards was carried upstairs at home he made the stretcher-bearers stop for a minute. Up came voices from down below.

'Five, that makes five of us in the family.'

'Yes, when you look at it that way –'

'Yes it's a record, no doubt. Like those families who lost all their sons in the war, five men, seven men, and death duties payable on all estates.'

'Oh, we're better off than the war-bereaved.' That was his wife's voice. 'Redundancy is not killed in action.'

'It can feel like it,' said Tom's brother.

That was how he found out that since his fall two men and two women of his family had been made redundant besides Johnny, Cora's husband. Incidentally, as he found out later, another relative, a woman personnel manager, had herself made redundant twenty-eight men in her office.

* * *

Tom confided in his day nurse, Julia: 'I fall in love easily and often. When I am overwhelmed with love I am in a state of complete enchantment, forgetting all the previous times I have fallen into raptures over a woman. At such times it doesn't matter who my wife is, what she knows, what she thinks. Nothing matters but the woman of my current obsession, of my dreams.'

It was four in the afternoon. Julia was preparing to go home. The night nurse came on at eight.

'And who is the lucky girl of the moment?' said Julia.

'No one. With a damaged spine and a broken leg and my ribs all in pieces, I may never love again.'

'With all those glamorous film stars in your life?' said Julia. 'I wouldn't believe it.' She took away his tea tray.

'I may never direct another film. Do you think anybody would put their money into a redundant director?'

'Personality is everything,' said Julia.

'I suppose you've got a husband,' said Tom.

'Yes, and three children.'

'Three lovely children.'

'I didn't say lovely.'

'You're the only young mother I've met who hasn't. What does your husband do?'

'He's second mechanic in a garage.'

'Is his job safe?'

'Oh, I think so. He's very well thought of.'

Her uniform was mauve, faintly striped with white. Her hair was blonde with darkened roots. Her figure was good, not too thin, it looked as if it had had three children. Her eyes were light blue. She was nothing special. For that, he liked her. He liked her in the way he had taken to that girl in France who was making hamburgers and sandwiches on a camping site, and who had struck his imagination so that he had kept her in his thoughts for weeks. He drafted a film script about her. He called her Jeanne. He got a screen-writer to do a first screenplay. He raised the money. He was directing the film when he fell. All of which had started with the sight of a nondescript sort of girl in a pink overall on a summer campsite in the Haute Savoie, making up sandwich packs for the campers and frying hamburgers for them on a rigged-up spirit stove, in a space so small that only the French could have contrived to cook in it. Tom had no further interest at all in the girl, except that glimpse. She would never know she had inspired a film, first in the hands of one and now in the hands of another director.

Julia had gone home. Tom was left brooding on the film in the hands of another director, so working himself up. He now recalled the plans he had made and the vow he had taken before he underwent the operation that followed his fall. The plans, the vow, were absurd. He had made them in a state of shock. No wonder he hadn't been able to recall what they were when he saw Fortescue-Brown. The plans were to trace the hamburger girl on the campsite, with the aid of Fortescue-Brown, and give her anonymously, just make her a gratuitous gift of, an enormous fortune. He would have to acquire a fortune speedily with the aid of Fortescue-Brown, probably by murdering his wife Claire in some undetectable way, and inheriting her money.

Tom was aghast. The film script, which conveyed an

element of this scenario, was one thing; real life another. The main development of Tom's scheme was of course the murder. In the actual film the girl's benefactor had been rich already.

Did I really make such a vow, such plans, there in the nuns' hospital? Tom wondered. I must, he thought, have been very much under shock, very drugged. He thought guiltily of Claire, his nice kind wife. What would Fortescue-Brown have thought if he had elaborated the plan? He would have thought Tom mad. But of course the film was non-realistic, so full of images of that old man in the years following that gesture in defiance of his natural fears – trying to trace the young girl again for love, all for love –

The door opened. Claire, in skin-tight blue jeans, a shirt and two strings of pearls came in, followed by Johnny Carr, his son-in-law, who had just been made redundant by the paint firm.

Claire said, 'Johnny's come to see you, Tom. He won't stay long.'

Tom said, 'If you think I am a stone that you shouldn't leave unturned, you are wasting your time.'

'Tom,' he said, 'all that matters is how are you feeling?'

'Ah.'

His visit to Tom was indeed by way of a probe, and Johnny Carr was furious to be confronted with so indelicate a truth. He might have known that Cora's father was unlikely to be mellowed by suffering. And anyway, Claire had urged the visit far too soon: 'He could certainly help you, Johnny. He knows so many people.'

As it was, Tom said, 'Redundancy comes to this: Nobody fires a man if he is exceptionally good, unless the whole outfit closes down. Your paint concern going out of business?'

'No, just restructuring. But forget it, Tom –'

'Very well.'

Johnny had put on his best business suit, which he intended to keep in first-class condition for interviews. After visiting Tom he went home, took off the special suit, and put on his clothes.

'How's Pa?' said Cora.

'He seems to be all right.'

'All right!' said Cora, who was fond of her father. 'What do you mean, all right, when he has broken bones all over his body. Sixty-three and nurses day and night. Poor Pa, he's lucky to be alive. He works so hard, he puts everything he's got into films. He lives films. How can he be all right?'

'He'd like to see you,' said Johnny.

'Did he say so?'

'Yes.'

'Should I just go, or make an appointment?' said Cora.

'Make an appointment with his secretary,' suggested Johnny. 'Mentally, he is back at work.'

Cora just went. Her job in France was over and she was back in the office at Channel Four. She was tall, with light brown hair and sometimes wore large gold-rimmed spectacles. She had long legs, narrow hips and, when she visited Tom, was dressed in a short skirt and sweater, both in turquoise blue. Cora was twenty-nine.

She bore no resemblance whatsoever to her mother, Katia, who was a different sort of beauty, of Bulgarian-Polish origin. Katia was dark and bold, now well into her second marriage. She had 'served her time' she said; she had paid her debt to society with the film director Tom Richards, and was now getting back her breath with the highly-paid managing director of a building society, definitely a non-genius, but not, like Tom, a big spender.

Cora sat in the bedside-chair while the day nurse, Julia, pulled Tom's sheets straight and puffed the pillows.

'We'd like some tea,' said Tom.

Julia looked at her watch.

'Never mind the time. We'd like some tea.'

Cora was so beautiful, Tom wished she were not his daughter. He looked and looked. He had always been dazzled by Cora, always besotted, always protectively chaste so that he resented any other man who was not chaste with Cora, a string of men, culminating with Johnny, whom, like a fool, she had married. She had married him for his looks which were admittedly star quality; but marriage was not a film; Cora was not a director; she had cast him in the role of a husband and he was hopeless at it. In screenplays the husband has a script to go by. Johnny had next to none.

'Now he's out of work,' said Tom.

'Who is out of work?'

'Johnny.'

'Oh, Johnny. He's looking for another job. There are millions out of work.'

'How do you manage the household budget?'

'You sound like Mum. We haven't had much time to budget.'

'Oh, Cora, don't think of maintaining a man financially. I beg you, don't start.'

'For better or worse . . .' said Cora. 'You marry for better or worse. I came to see how you were,' Cora said. 'I don't want to talk about money, Pa.'

Julia brought in a tray of tea for two. Claire followed.

'You have a harem to wait on you, Tom,' she said. 'What more can you want?'

'My job,' said Tom. 'I want to finish my film but I can't do it. Someone else will do it. I'm in bed. I'm out of work.'

'There will be other films,' said Claire. 'There always have been.'

'My film is not replaceable,' said Tom. 'No work of art can be replaced. A work of art is like living people.'

CHAPTER THREE

It was left to Cora, the family beauty, to break the news to her father that he had to go back into hospital for a spinal operation. Cora was now in England, staying with Claire. She had no hope of a new contract with Channel Four, and her husband, handsome Johnny, three weeks after his redundancy was declared, had disappeared to India with his severance pay. Cora did not expect to see him again.

Before telling Tom what the specialist had said about his last X-rays, 'We have to operate on his back,' Cora told him about her husband's recent defection. She knew her father's rages, both of frustration and indignation, and decided that the latter, if exhausted first, might mitigate the former.

In his sober moments he agreed with Claire about the irascibility of his nature. Shortly after she had married him Claire observed, 'At times you act like a female hedgehog or a porcupine that has been sexually violated. All quills out, running around. A ravished porcupine, that's what you are at such times.'

'I know,' he said.

It was one of these attacks that Claire feared when she sent Cora into his bedroom to tell him that he had to go back to hospital. His sense of frustration was already near the boil since he couldn't yet walk properly. He crawled round the room slowly on an elbow-crutch. What incensed him most was when the visiting doctor told him how lucky he was to be alive, and reminded him that he had had a very bad fall.

Cora had a second mission: this was to tell Tom that the backers had withdrawn from the film. It was all folded up. The actors had gone home and Tom's worked-over script (for he never had a full-scale screen-writer, but himself wrote a lot of the films he directed) was lying downstairs in his study. He was still unable to go downstairs, but Claire felt he would have to know sooner or later, about the odd silence surrounding his proposed film provisionally entitled *The Hamburger Girl*. This provisional title was believed by all to be ambiguous and Tom certainly intended to change it. He was beginning to wonder about the lack of news, except for kind messages and flowers, from the area of that film. Cora knew he would choke with indignation when he heard it had folded up. And so she preferred to channel some of his ire into frustration first.

'Pa,' she said straight out, 'you need an operation on your spine next week, or you'll never walk right again. You're booked into the clinic.'

He was standing in the middle of his vast bedroom, leaning on two elbow-crutches.

To her amazement he said, 'All right.'

And when she went on to tell him about the work-stoppage on his film he said, 'Good. They would only have made a mess of it, Cora, without me.'

Claire and the nurse Julia, listening outside the bedroom door, were equally astonished.

'Tell me,' said Tom, 'how Johnny came to get to India. Who paid his fare? Did you?'

'In actual fact he took his redundancy money. It was quite a lot. Some thousands of pounds. Pa, I wasn't going to tell you, but he's gone.'

'What did he give to you before he left?'

'Nothing. He just took off.' Cora was crying now.

'Let him go,' said her father. 'Don't ever take him back. You can get a divorce. He wasn't ever your type and now you know it. Little egocentric swine.'

'Johnny was so good-looking,' said Cora. 'We made a fine couple, let's face it.'

'He would never have looks as good as yours. Let's face it,' said Tom to his really beautiful daughter. Only to see her move half across the room was an aesthetic delight.

'India,' she said. 'I said, Why India? He said, "To see my guru and a couple of temples in the south, and get lost to this materialistic hell. It's good-bye," he said, "for always. I'm not coming back. You can sell the sapphire ring. We can have a divorce any time you like. It's good-bye."'

'Why are you crying?' said Tom. 'With that sort, redundant is the very word. He is a non-necessary person.'

'He took only a few clothes,' said Cora. 'And I took

the rest and made a bonfire in the garden. I gave away his shoes, they were quite decent.'

'You did right. He'll want to come back. But don't have him. Did he take the door-key?'

'I suppose so.'

'Change the lock. He'll try to come back when his money's run out.'

'Oh I don't think he'll come back.'

'Take my advice,' said Tom. 'I am old and experienced. I am old. I was already twenty when I went to the opening night of *The Mousetrap*. Not only am I old enough to be your father, I am your father. You should listen to me.'

When the day began to wear away Cora got ready to leave. For Tom it was the worst time of every day since his accident. He would quote Longfellow to describe his evening mood:

> A feeling of sadness and longing,
> That is not akin to pain,
> And resembles sorrow only
> As the mist resembles the rain.

'I used to love this time of day,' he said before Cora left. 'The workers and staff would go home and the leading members of the cast and the directors would gather for a drink and discuss the day's work and plan the next day's. Now, it's only the depressing news on the television. Claire comes with a tray of terrible food. She thinks the new cook's wonderful. Her name is also

Claire. This cook-Claire should have her ass fired right out of our kitchen with her pretentious dishes, her goulash and her hogwash and her crème-caramels furnished by the supermarket. But Claire won't have a word said about her Hungarian cook. I don't care what she's suffered. Once a communist always a communist. She thinks she's our equal and we should be grateful for her presence under my roof.'

Cora sat down again. 'I'll stay with you. Let's have a drink,' she said.

'With all these antibiotics I'm not supposed to drink.'

'You can have one drink,' Cora said. 'The doctor told Claire and Claire told me.'

'My wife has a man,' said Tom.

'Claire has a man? Who?'

'I don't know.'

'But if it's true can you blame her,' Cora said. 'You have so many women.'

'That's part of my profession,' Tom said. 'Her profession is wife.'

'You don't sound very convincing.'

'Well I'm not convinced, really. I don't believe in convictions. They are generally hypocrisy.'

Claire was on the house-phone to Tom. 'A fax has just come in. They want to continue with the film with Stan Shephard directing. They must have found the money.'

'Let him direct, I've lost interest,' said Tom.

'Wait a minute,' said Claire, sensing he was about to hang up. 'They want to change the title to: *I'll Kill You If You Die*. I think that's rather –'

'No,' said Tom. 'The title of the movie is provisionally *The Hamburger Girl*. I don't like *I'll Kill You If You Die*. It ties down the meaning to a single incident, a single phase in the film. Tell them No.'

'From what they say they want to reconstruct the film in that sense. Do you want me to bring up the fax?'

'No. Just reply No.'

'No what? No to the whole film, no to the new director or just no to the title?'

'No to everything.'

'You can't do that. They have rights to the film. They have script rights, title rights, director rights. You know they have.'

'Do they ask how I'm keeping?'

'Oh yes, they say they hope you're improving.'

'If they have rights to everything, why are they faxing me?'

'Out of courtesy I suppose,' said Claire.

'Oh, no, they're not. Oh, no. On second thoughts, don't reply. Don't answer. If they have all these rights they won't bother me again. If they don't they'll write again. You should ask Fortescue-Brown the lawyer in any case. He got up the contract, let him get on with it.'

This time he hung up before Claire could say a word. The nurse, Julia, had a large over-toothed smile on her face. 'The good news,' she said, 'is that you don't have to undergo another operation. There was a misdiagnosis, too hasty, but fortunately the surgeon noticed in time. It was a question of the X-rays.'

'Is this the surgeon like a ghost who never comes

into a room and never goes out of it but just materialises and vanishes?'

'That's him. Mr. Gladstone Smith.'

'Oh, a Mr. Smith. Does he know what he's talking about?'

'He certainly does. You don't need to go back to hospital. You're going to be all right.'

'As soon as I hear a bit of news these days,' said Tom, 'someone comes along to contradict it. My film was cancelled now it's going ahead. My son-in-law was looking for a job but now he's left my daughter and gone for a holiday in India. First I had to go back to hospital and now I don't.'

'That's life,' said Julia.

'No, it's not ordinary life. But let me tell you that for people in the film business, yes, it is life. Nothing with us is consistent.'

Tom's daughter by his second marriage, Marigold, and her husband James, lived (when he wasn't on his literary travels) in a large cottage in a village in Surrey. They were both very serious people – too serious for Tom, but who was to say that he was the just arbiter of other people's character? Simply because he was always ready to assume that part, and others only too ready to listen to him with dazzled conviction is not to say that Tom was always right (although generally there was something in what he said). When James was away Marigold lived alone, but at this moment she had James's elder brother, Ralph and his wife Ruth to stay with her. Ralph and Ruth had come down from London at Marigold's invitation to get over the trauma of Ralph's redundancy and to sort themselves out. They were in their early thirties, with two children away at school. The fact of the approaching school holidays gave Marigold a sense of confidence that, because of the children coming home, the couple could not stay with her very long as otherwise they might have been tempted to.

In the meantime Marigold indulged her gift for philosophising, if not sermonising. After supper, the very first night of their stay, she spoke.

The two in-laws sat on a dismal blue sofa, side by side. Marigold, worthy as any woman or man in the works of George Eliot, unlovely, graceless, sat in an upright chair opposite. (How had Tom managed to conceive her? And Claire, so emotionally imaginative?) Marigold spoke:

'Perhaps nobody,' Marigold said, 'should take on responsibilities which would demand more expenditure than would be gained from the dole and the income support schemes. Full pay has a surplus which should not be used for necessities such as house purchases or school fees unless a private income covers those expenditures. In other words, if all lived austerely, redundancy would bring no shock to the person or the family. My point number two is that employed persons should have an alternative source of income, for example, the income deriving from the invested surplus of a good salary not put to full expenditure. My third point is that every breadwinner should have in mind if not at hand an alternative career of a robust nature to step into if the first one fails.'

(Perhaps Marigold's only resemblance to Tom was that she indulged in monologues. But was this inherited or only copied?)

Ralph said, 'It's too late for me, all this advice.' He had been a manager of liaison personnel in a vast branch of an international electronics firm. He had been laid off with twenty-three others. Ralph looked at his watch, saw that it was six o'clock, time for a drink, went over to the drinks tray and helped himself to a gin and tonic. He said, 'Can I get you girls anything?'

'Scotch and soda,' said Ruth.

'A diet Cola,' said Marigold, who looked decidedly put out by Ralph's proprietary actions. 'I hope,' she said, 'you have signed on with a B.A. and let them have your C.V. with a claim for A.P.L.'

'What are B.A., A.P.L.?' said Ruth.

'Benefits Agency; Accreditation of Prior Learning. C.V. means curriculum vitae which means – '

'I know that one,' said Ruth.

'So do I,' said Ralph. 'If you mean am I applying, or looking, for other jobs, well, yes, at least I mean to do so.'

'You need to find your L.A.'s U.B.O. and perhaps put in for some E.T.'

'Oh certainly,' said Ralph, 'every time.'

Marigold looked disappointed. 'Do you know what these letters stand for? Of course you don't. L.A. is Local Authority, U.B.O. is the unemployment benefit office of your L.A. E.T. is Employment Training which you will no doubt need if you are adaptable to a new occupation. These terms of reference should be known to you. They are known to me so why shouldn't they be known to you?'

Ruth said, 'One lives and learns. In the meantime we have my pay to live on.'

'Still you should have some I.S.' (By this Marigold meant Income Support but Ralph and Ruth enquired no further.)

[35]

'I saw in the papers,' Ruth said, 'that your father had a fall. How is he?'

'Still physically impaired, but otherwise more exasperating than ever. He's home now, keeping to his room for the time being. I suppose the nursing home was glad to get rid of him. He made passes at the youngest nurses and cheeked up to the older ones. I was there in his room when one of these older women came to check his temperature and so on. She asked him, "Have your bowels acted?" He said, "Yes, have yours?" That was the sort of thing. I'm sorry for my mother, coping with him at home. There's a nurse, of course, eating into the family fortunes. My half-sister Cora eggs him on. She rang me up. She said, "I've told Pa to keep on the night nurse too if he wants it. That's what money is for."'

'Will he direct films again?' said Ralph.

'Maybe and maybe not. He's writing a lot at the moment. Probably a film script. But there's no knowing what the shock has done to his abilities. I hope he has an insurance and an S.D.A., otherwise –'

'S.D.A.?' said Ruth.

'Severe Disablement Allowance,'' Marigold pronounced slowly to Ruth, as if to a cretin. 'Otherwise my mother will have to support him.'

'Oh but she's so wealthy,' said Ralph.

'You'd be surprised,' said Marigold, 'to know how much dependent members of a family can deplete a fortune.'

'Oh, obviously,' Ruth said. 'But look, those Blantyres from upstate New York are very, very, well off.'

'And flourishing,' said Ralph. 'Blantyre Biscuits Inc.

are away ahead. Surely your mother has suffered no loss by her marriage, no deprivation. She's still a Blantyre with Blantyre money and a famous husband.'

'There comes a time,' said Marigold. 'However, there comes a time when one has to see things *sub specie aeternitatis.* Which means,' she said, turning to Ruth, 'under the light of eternity. That is what my parents now have to do. Examine their utility, their service ability, their accountability, their duties and commitments, instead of respectively womanising and manising as they have done in the past, as they continue to do, and as they no doubt mean to do.'

'What else should they do?' said Ruth.

'They could get a divorce, for a start,' said Marigold.

'Oh no,' protested Ralph and Ruth almost simultaneously.

'My mother has a man,' said Marigold. 'I think his name's Charlie. The phone rang several times when I was there. Once my mother ran to pick up the receiver; she said, "That's Charlie." Evidently it was Charlie. And when I asked her how did she know it was Charlie's call, she said, "I know his ring." That means she's besotted.'

CHAPTER FIVE

Tom's room overlooked a garden of twisting gravel
pathways, grass, shrubbery and trees. There were no
flower-beds. His furniture and part of the floor were
covered with books and papers. It was a large room,
meant for himself and Claire who, since Tom's accident,
had made way for a night nurse who was lodged in an
adjacent dressing room. Now Claire was back in the
dressing room, the night nurse being unnecessary.
However, Tom had the huge bedroom to himself for his
exercises and massages by the day nurse Julia. In part of
the great room was a space where a sofa, some comfortable chairs and a table of drinks and some smaller tables
were disposed, and here Tom received his visitors who
stepped over the books to greet him, shake his hand, or
hug him as the case might be. As his injuries improved,
the more frequently did he hold court. 'My bedroom,' he
boasted to Claire, 'is the in-place to be.'

Marigold's brother-in-law Ralph and his wife Ruth

were among his visitors one time when Tom was alone. They were on their way home having cut short their stay with Marigold to one night. Tom had not seen them for at least two years, since Marigold's wedding. He had taken Marigold up the aisle on his arm and was aware of James's tribe in their pews. Later, at the feast, he had met them all, and perceived that they were a clever lot. He liked Marigold's husband, a journalist at that time, and only hoped he could make Marigold relax. Now he was a travel-writer, not that he ever took Marigold with him on his travels. It looked bad. But James's brother Ralph was one of the family he had thought amiable and felt easy with. Claire had taken to the wife, Ruth, a shapely girl.

Claire ushered them in to Tom, who raised his elbow-crutch in greeting and turned off the television. It was exactly six o'clock in the evening. 'Have a drink,' said Tom. 'Claire, give them a drink.'

Claire's charm oozed out towards them. She was always extremely well groomed with a shiny blonde head, clear eyebrows and an oval made-up face. Her neat coat and skirt were dark, her silk shirt white. She prepared the drinks with a flash of long silver fingernails.

'You have troubles,' said Tom to Ralph. 'I hear you've lost your job.'

'You have worse troubles,' said Ralph. 'Tell us how you are.'

'Some days better than others. I take pills. The physiotherapist comes. I do exercises. Sooner or later I'll be back to normal. At my age it might be later rather than sooner.'

'It must have been a frightful shock,' said Ruth.

'He's lucky to be alive,' Claire said.

'Being alive is not always lucky. But in my case it is because I enjoy my life. Can you two stay a few nights?'

'Of course they can,' said Claire. 'We've already arranged it.'

'Because,' said Tom, 'I have to go to bed early. I have supper in bed. Julia, my nurse, has to be home by seven-thirty. She has three children and a nice husband to go to. But I'd like to have a chance to talk to you tomorrow in the day time.'

'We could all look in and see you later tonight,' Claire said.

'No, I'll drop off to sleep after the news.'

'Oh Tom,' said Claire, 'you must try to get out of that habit of going to sleep so early. It'll make you old. Look at the politicians of sixty-three at the height of their careers.'

'They make me want to sleep all the more, especially during their interviews. No eloquence, no gifts at all. And the show generally so shabbily produced. Evil lighting. Spiteful close-ups. All that. How I long for some literate entertainment. I used to know lots of older writers, thinkers and theatre people. They are all dead or nearly, now. The century is getting old, very old. Old with all the faults of old age; especially what Eliot called "the desperate exercise of failing power". You see it everywhere. It's grotesque.'

'Have you any idea,' Tom asked Julia when she brought him his supper on a tray, 'who is dining down there to-night?'

'The two new guests,' said Julia. 'And Claire and Charlie.'

'Describe Charlie. Is he small and fat?'

'No, tall and manly. Very good-looking, in fact. Don't work yourself up, Tom. I'm sure he's only a friend.'

'Will he stay here for the night?'

'I don't think so.' In the kitchen Claire the cook and Dollie, the maid, were debating that very point. No extra bed made up in the single room, nothing arranged for his breakfast. 'We feel he's only here for dinner, to make an extra man.'

'How good of you to get me all this information,' said Tom. 'Did he bring flowers?'

'No, no flowers. Perhaps he'll send them tomorrow. They often send flowers after a party.'

'Does he seem to have that much savvy?'

'I don't know. I haven't had the opportunity to judge him close-up,' said Julia who was putting on her out-door things. 'Will I wait for the tray?' she said.

'No, Claire will come up and take it away later on. Good-night, Julia.'

'See you in the morning.'

In the morning Tom's first visitor was Ralph. It was nine-thirty. The bed was made and Tom was sitting in his chair with his legs up on an orthopaedic rest.

'Apart from this disability,' said Tom, 'we are putting a lift in the house, so that we can get up and down. As it is, I expect to do the stairs within a month, six weeks. That's what they say.'

'If there's anything I can do ...'

'Nothing, thanks. I suppose you are busy looking for another job.'

'I'm going to be active in that area. I believe it's more exhausting looking for work than doing it.'

'Did your redundancy come as a shock?'

'Yes. Although I might have expected it. I was truly under shock. From one moment to the next I had status, a settled income, then nothing. But I pulled myself together enough to make a deal with the firm. That included the severance handshake and the hush-money.'

'What hush-money?'

'Not to reveal the secrets of the firm to the next employer.'

'That should be a difficult promise to keep. You would be bound to use your utmost knowledge in a new job.'

'Yes, it's an impossible promise to keep. It's only that once having signed an agreement one doesn't actually go round selling knowledge as a separate item. Especially in the electronics business, knowledge is valuable.'

'Knowledge is always valuable,' said Tom. He was looking at Ralph with new eyes: check shirt, smart, loose country jacket, slim twill trousers, good shoes. An open face with a flush of pink, wide grey eyes, plenty of sleek dark hair, hands in good shape. Ralph had been envied for his earning power by his brother, Tom's son-in-law, who wrote travel books but lived above his income, largely, now, on Marigold's money which, through Claire, was considerable. Ralph was no longer a financial prodigy. He was out of work, probably for a long time, possibly for ever.

'You have youth on your side,' Tom said.

'You mean I can switch my brain to something else?' Ralph said.

'Yes, that's one of the things I mean.'

'I can tell you from personal experience,' Ralph said, 'that redundancy causes sexual disaster. It causes anxiety and inadequate erections.'

'These are early days,' said Tom. 'You'll get over that hang-up in a few weeks.'

'According to statistics, no. Apparently the phenomenon of male redundancy is frequently accompanied by a brusque fall in sexual activity and reduced desire with the impossibility of having a complete erection. I read an article about it, and now I've found it's so.'

'It will pass. It's only the result of shock. Don't try.'

'That's what Ruth says. She's very understanding about it.'

'Lucky fellow.'

Julia came in with her many-toothed smile, fresh in her mauve and white uniform. She had a small medicine glass containing a number of antibiotic pills in one hand and a glass of water in another. Tom swallowed the pills and washed them down. 'Beastly stuff,' he said.

Julia bent her smile on Ralph as she went out.

'Good-looking,' said Ralph.

'Toothy.'

'Toothy women are said to be sexy.'

'I wouldn't know. She has a husband and three children. At the moment I'm not sexually active, but I have the most intense desires. Normally, I have a great many women.'

'So I've heard. Hadn't I better go?'

'No, don't go. Mornings are the most boring times for me. In the afternoons I read and in the evenings I watch something on the television, idiot-box though it is, or a video, sometimes with Claire. Unless you're in a hurry –'

'No hurry at all. I came really to tell you that Claire has been awfully good to us. Last night she gave Ruth a cheque for five thousand pounds. We are not at the moment in need but it is acceptable and wonderful of Claire, considering we are not very closely related.'

'Claire is very rich,' Tom said. 'Claire is also very generous with her money. I'm glad to say.'

'I wanted to make sure you approve.'

'Oh, I approve of everything Claire does. I spend my life approving of Claire. We have been married over a quarter of a century.'

'You seem to have spent your life being a success.'

'It's not enough,' said Tom. 'Now I'm redundant.'

'Not permanently. To be in your position must be a great satisfaction,' said Ralph. He got up and went to the window, apparently to look at the garden below. It was a fine day, a fact which did not seem to be of much comfort to Ralph, Tom thought; quite the reverse, perhaps.

'When I was a young writer, when I first wrote and directed,' Tom said, 'I had a great many friends older than myself, some a little older, some much older. Now that I need them to come and visit me, to pass by and talk to me, most of them are dead. If Auden were alive he would have come to see me in his shabby clothes. Wystan said he always felt his parents should provide his clothes and couldn't shake off that feeling even now when he was an adult. He liked to spend his money on food. Wystan gave good dinners. I remember in the sixties when he lived in Manhattan in a near-slum in St. Mark's Place what fine food he would sit one down to. At least, his man friend Chester Kallman used to cook that delicious food. Wystan kept his new work under the sofa. He would scramble under the sofa to bring out his batch of poems to read to me. Chester would come out of the kitchen into the room with a red face, wearing his cooking apron. In fact I seldom saw Chester without his apron. Even in Austria the last time I went to see them, Chester was wearing that big kitchen apron. He made Austrian food – dumplings, but so special. He was more than a cook, however, he was a good librettist.

'If Graham Greene were alive he would have looked in to see me, perhaps not in hospital but certainly here at home. Sex was his main subject, when you met him at least to start with. He had a mix-up of women and felt guilty the whole time. Without girls I think he couldn't have carried on. He needed it for his writing. Graham would have sent me a dozen bottles of rare wine or champagne. He would have come for an evening's talk and drink if he had known I was stuck in this bedroom. He would talk about sex always as if it was the forbidden fruit of the tree of knowledge. Sex and desire and the hazards thereof, such as divorce and venereal disease. I tried to get him on to religion but he was chary of that subject, Catholicism. He believed in it without swallowing everything, which is possible, and in fact more widely practised than one might think. In fact he couldn't not believe, in spite of himself.

'So much for his beliefs, but in some ways he had a bureaucratic conception of Catholic doctrine, but so do many Catholics including the present Pope. Greene never called me Tom, by the way. It was always "Richards". But he called Claire "Claire" of course. Which reminds me of Allen Tate another Catholic who was keen on women. Have you heard of Tate?'

'No,' said Ralph. 'Unless you mean an American writer, I seem to remember . . .'

'You remember right. He was an American poet, critic, and Anglophile. He went to see Pius XII in 1957. He told me how it went. Allen said, "Your Holiness, the English and American Catholic Bishops are feeling uneasy about the Index of Forbidden Books. After the acts of censorship under totalitarianism the intelligent Catholic laity want more democratic freedom."

'"Ah yes," said Pius, "Maritain was here last week with that problem. Greene came about it recently. How many children, – nephews, do you have?"

'Allen told him how many.

'The Pope said, "Here are four rosaries. The black ones are for boys, the white for girls." End of audience.'

'Was that the Pope before this?'

'No it was actually five Popes ago.'

'Don't your friends ring you up?'

'Yes, they do. Claire takes the calls. I don't always want to talk. People can send me a fax. They do, quite often. I don't always want to reply. They want to know if I'll be ready to give a lecture on film-making at some university in six months' time, they want to know if they have my permission to change some paragraphs in my film script, they want to know if they can come and see me. What do I say? – I could say "I've got a back-ache. Disintegrate. Drop dead. Do what you damn well like." If it was Louis MacNeice I'd let him come and see me. I worked with him several times on the Third Programme when it and the radio really meant something. But Louis is dead.'

'Don't you think you should write your memoirs?'

'I'm too young at sixty-three to write my memoirs. I'm still in the act of creating memoirs, which is right. But just at the moment, as you can imagine, my experiences of historic moments are limited if not nil. One never knows, of course, until one looks back.'

Ralph was still looking out of the window. 'There's an extremely beautiful girl,' he said, 'coming up the garden path.'

'That will be my daughter Cora by my first marriage. Half-sister to Marigold. You would hardly know it. Cora increases in beauty every year. Hadn't you better be joining the others?'

Ralph went quite quickly, obviously hoping to encounter Cora. The girl, however, came up by the back stairs to Tom's room holding a single flower, a large yellow daisy, in a slim vase, her offering of the day.

'Can I have my lunch with you, Pa?'

'Fine. Tell Claire I want it served on the Sèvres china.'

'Oh, no, she won't do that.' Cora looked over to a table where about a dozen ordinary plates were piled up. 'You can break these any time you like,' said Cora.

'I don't want to break that ghastly crockery. To relieve my feelings I want the best china in the house.'

Julia came in with a thermometer and some pills.

'See you later,' said Cora.

Tom had an instinct of disquiet. He felt that Cora would run into Ralph, and after that some drama might happen. He knew himself to be jealous for Cora, and didn't like the idea of her solving the redundant Ralph's sexual problems.

'Will these pills make me impotent?' he said to Julia.

'Impotent? Shouldn't do.'

'I miss sex.'

'You mustn't strain yourself, anyway. Think of something else.'

CHAPTER SIX

Cora's life had been fairly easy for the first nineteen years. She was always much admired for her good looks and her ability at riding, swimming and tennis. She was average at school work. When her father left home she was too young to notice his absence, which in any case was almost a constant factor. The difficulties of her life had started when she was nineteen. It was obvious that she would try the acting profession and through Tom's influence she had many opportunities. She had the looks, was photogenic, but she didn't have any acting imagination in her. She treated this fact, as she did most difficulties, as an inanimate obstacle to be overcome: this, besides her beauty, was her strength. She had a perfect form, a fresh, charming face, good hands, grey-green eyes and a mane of brown hair. She walked like a leopard. Tom doted on her.

'What a pity she can't act,' he was heard to say. 'She has so much else. But acting is an art that you cannot really learn. A certain amount of training might improve the actor's art, but essentially to be an actor you have to be born with the whole stock and merchandise built-in. Acting is fundamentally the art of hypocrisy. Nothing can put it there. Cora's no good even for television commercials. She has spontaneous expressions on her face but she can't put them on. An art is something you bring with you into the world, just as Cora brought her beauty.'

So far was Cora from any art of dissimulation, that she was at a positive disadvantage in some of her relationships, especially with men and employers. She could not fall in love intensely or long enough to match the desire she aroused in men. Out of boredom, she could not stick at any job, even being photographed for magazine covers. She was now twenty-nine, unemployed and more beautiful in her appearance than ever, the apple of her father's eye.

It was Marigold who joyfully brought to Claire and Tom the news that Cora and Ralph were having an affair. It was not yet two weeks since Ralph had first seen Cora from Tom's bedroom window. Claire, Tom and Marigold were taking drinks in the sitting room portion of Tom's room when Marigold came out with the news.

'But,' said Tom wildly, almost hopefully, 'Ralph has a sexual hang-up as a consequence of being made redundant. It's a common phenomenon apparently throughout Europe.'

'Not with Cora, he hasn't got a hang-up. I know,' said Marigold.

Marigold knows everything, Tom thought. How?

Evidently by making it her business to know. That's how people know things.

'And,' said Marigold, 'he has bought Cora a gold watch of some extremely expensive make. He bought it using part of the money Mother gave him, I know.'

(She knows . . .)

'If it helps him over the hump I don't blame him,' said Claire. 'That's what the money was for.'

'It isn't any function of Cora to help anyone over their hump,' Tom said.

'What about his wife,' said Claire. 'Does Ruth know?'

'I don't know,' said Marigold.

(Something she *doesn't* know . . . Not yet.)

'Not yet,' Marigold added, innocently.

Try as he might, Tom was not fond of his daughter by Claire. Even Claire was disconcerted at times by the way Marigold had developed.

'Ruth is bound to suspect something,' Marigold went on. 'He can't explain his absences by the excuse of job-hunting all the time.'

'Let the thing blow over,' Tom said. 'It will certainly blow over. He'll probably find a job. He's a very able young man.'

'There are plenty of able young men,' said Marigold. 'And Ralph won't find a job so long as Mother gives him fat cheques.'

'It's my money, not yours,' Claire said without vehemence. She was accustomed to use this phrase to her family. She uttered it frequently.

'It's a question of what's good for Ralph. His marriage. And what's good for Cora,' said Marigold. 'From that point of view it's a moral question.'

Sooner or later, thought Tom, Marigold had to make it out to be a moral question. Sooner or later.

'I don't know about a moral question,' Claire said, 'but Cora shouldn't break up a young married couple. She's old enough to know better.'

'She is so irresistibly lovely,' Tom said, 'that temptation is different, more pressing by far, for Cora than for either of you. You can't possibly blame Cora if a man loses his head over her.'

Claire looked at her watch. 'It's time for your injection,' she said. She went over to the door of the adjacent room and, opening it, found Julia preparing her shot. Turning to Marigold, Claire said, 'Let's go down.'

'Put on a CD,' Tom said to Julia. 'Find Mahler's Symphony No.1, New York Philharmonic.' She gave him his injection, found the disc and put it on.

Next morning, Sunday, came the relief nurse.

Tom's incoming calls were controlled by the house so that he shouldn't be worried by unwanted callers, but he had a direct outgoing line. He dialled Cora's number and got an answering machine on which he left a message for her to call him back. He felt guilty about his wish to interfere in Cora's life, but the desire was stronger than the guilt. He wasn't at all sure what he would say to Cora by way of enquiry, warning, deprecation of her presumed affair with Ralph. She was getting a divorce from Johnny. She was free. She was twenty-nine.

'What's going on downstairs?' he asked the nurse,

who was making the bed with a flourish of sheets that looked like a ship in full sail.

'Your wife is preparing the vegetables because it's Sunday and there's no cook.'

'She likes to cook.'

'She told me she hates doing the veg. but she likes to cook, as you say. I offered to help because, after all, your meals are involved, but Claire wouldn't let me.' The nurse's long arms threw the final cover in the air and landed it neatly on the bed.

'Who's coming to lunch – anybody?'

'I don't know. It looks like company's expected.'

'Find out,' said Tom.

A knock on the door. The masseur, a squat, powerful Greek came in with a bag of ointments. His name was Ron. Tom lay down on the orthopaedic chaise-longue while Ron kneaded, pummelled and rubbed for three-quarters of an hour, during which Tom forgot to brood on Cora's affair and who was lunching with Claire.

'This physical experience is almost a spiritual one,' he observed to Ron.

'I hear this before, it's well-known,' said Ron. 'Many persons feel they relax in the spirit from massage.'

'What is the difference between body and spirit?' said Tom.

'There is a difference but both are very alike, you know,' said Ron.

'At least, interdependent I should say,' Tom said.

It was not to be expected that Tom would be sympathetically inclined towards the substitute director of his film. The man came to see Tom to explain his method, which he called his aesthetic strategy, thus outrageing Tom from the start. The new director was moreover about thirty-five, far too young in Tom's view. Everything was now being done at a speed which was strained even for the film industry, apparently to recoup the damage done to the project by Tom's fall. The title of the film was now to be neither *The Hamburger Girl* nor *I'll Kill You If You Die*. It was to be *The Lunatic Fringe*, to which Tom objected for obscure reasons. He took the title, the breathless course of events, and the ever-recurring phrase 'cost-effective' as a personal insult. 'This is too much,' Tom said; 'one title last week and a different one this week. I'm aware that we live in a world of rapid change. Only last week my wife was complaining that her shares in Barings Bank had gone down the drain, and this week her shares have not gone down the drain. But this is too much. You can't change the title without changing the film altogether. I won't agree to it. Tell them I'll sue.'

It would be useless to give here the name of the latest director because, not surprisingly, he was out of the show in less than a month, but not before Tom had been considerably upset by the cancellation of the contract of two young male actors.

'I chose them,' Tom said with shrill emphasis, 'for their looks.'

'Ah!' said the upstart, 'you can't hire actors mainly for their looks.' He looked for support at the casting director, a mature woman, whom he had brought along with him on this occasion. But the casting director had eyes only for Tom, whom she adored.

'They are adequate actors,' said Tom, 'but more important, they look like the actors who play the parts of their respective parents.'

'Uncannily like,' said the casting director.

'Plausibility, my dear man,' said Tom, 'is what you aim for as a basis for a film. Achieve that basic something, and you can then do what you like. You can make the audience go along with you, anywhere, everywhere. It is extremely difficult to cast parents and their adult children, except in a homogeneous society. To me,' he hammered on with justified pride and no tact, 'it is not good enough to cast sons and daughters totally different from at least one of the parents, or parents who have no pretence of a family likeness with their children, as you see in so many films. In Scandinavia, of course, the casting is easier. Bergman's blood-relations, for instance, always look like blood-relations.'

When the new director shortly flopped out Tom tried to get back his original 'blood-relations' into the act. He was not successful because the screenplay had been changed to eliminate them. They were unnecessary.

Tom had money in the film. 'Call Fortescue-Brown,' he told Claire. 'I want to withdraw from the film altogether. It's no longer mine. I wash my hands of it. I withdraw my name. I want my money back.'

'You could go and direct in a wheel chair,' said Claire. 'You'll be about in a wheel chair before long. We could easily arrange for you to go on the set a few hours a day.'

'I wouldn't dream of it,' Tom said.

However, he did dream of it. He was now able to leave his room and get himself wheeled into the house's new service lift. Claire fussed greatly, getting him into the car with his folding chair at the back. The driver. The instructions. He suspected that Claire was glad to get him out of the way for hours on end.

'Where's my great crane?' said Tom. 'What have you done with our Chapman crane?'

'Tom,' said his assistant. 'You can't go up in that crane any more.'

'I want to know where it is?'

'We rented it out. Anyway, you can't even use the dolly just yet. Do you really think they'd let you sit at those angles?'

'They say that it was being at maximum tilt that saved me in my fall from the crane. Something scientific about the angle of the fall. Pilots who crash go up again and fly. The crane –'

'Oh, no, Tom, there is no crane. You can't have any more trips on the crane. The insurance would never take you on, even if we would.'

'Who is we?'

'All of us. The crew. The production people. No crane. To be honest, we sold it.'

'I need an amplifier. I need a lot of hand-cameras and camera rests. There is frequent sprinting towards the object in this movie. I don't want you to be afraid of wrecking cameras. The man has to sprint and stop just inches away.'

'All that's been done already, Tom. At least a lot of it's been done. There are plenty of cameras.'

'There is all the difference,' Tom proceeded, 'between a dedicated cameraman and a cameraman full-stop. You need inspiration. Where have we got to?'

[58]

'There's had to be a lot of re-editing, Tom. We're in a state of transition.'

'I want the screenplay, my screenplay,' Tom said. 'I want to take it home and see what you've changed. I want some sign of inspiration. Do you know what inspiration is? It is the descent of the Holy Spirit. I was talking to a Cardinal the other day. He said there was a theory that the ages of the Father and the Son were over and we were approaching the age of the Holy Spirit, or as we used to say, Ghost. The century is old, very old. Call my car.'

'The screenplay, Tom,' said his assistant director, 'is very tentative just at this moment.' But he gave Tom a rough-handled copy. Tom waved to the assembled crew as he was wheeled out.

'Take it easy, Tom.' 'Great to see you, Tom.' 'Keep it up, Tom.'

'I'll be back tomorrow,' said Tom. 'Punctually at eight.'

CHAPTER SEVEN

A sixth sense, based on experience, told Claire that Tom would persuade himself that he should come to the rescue of Ruth while her husband, Ralph, was occupied with Cora. In fact, up to his accident, consciously or otherwise, he had made a speciality of the wives of redundant men, succeeding in about half of the cases. In arriving at this statistic Claire took into account that a film director holds a special attraction for women. And to be honest, thought Claire, the reason why I stick by him is that he's an interesting film director. She was in her mid-fifties. Most of her friends, male and female, were now on to their third marriage. Tom was her first and although she knew why she was still attached to him, Claire never wondered why he remained with her. She was rich, discreet about her men, tolerant of his women, a good hostess and good-looking. Why should a husband over sixty want to leave her?

And in fact, Tom had no such intention. He was

courting Ruth who still was not aware of her husband's affair with Cora. She only knew that Ralph was frequently away looking for a job, having interviews all over England, and that Tom was extremely friendly and helpful. Tom was not yet up to the real, the physical, part of a love affair, which misled her considerably and in fact induced in her sentimental feelings for Tom. His wheel-chair visits and his flowers made her happy. He brought her a bracelet worked in white, red and yellow gold. She had tight-fitting jeans and long blonde hair. Tom thought of her as the hamburger girl. He thought of her as being in her early twenties although she was well into her thirties.

Claire soon got knowledge of this courtship from her daughter Marigold. As usual Claire infuriated her daughter by being absent-minded about such knowledge.

'Don't you care?' said Marigold, with a little shriek accompanying the word 'care'.

'No,' said Claire. 'You know I don't.'

'It's a family matter,' Marigold said.

'That's why it bores me even more than your father's other affairs.'

'Why don't you divorce him?' Marigold intoned.

'You always ask that. And I ask in return why don't you divorce your own husband? He's never at home.'

'He can't write travel books and stay at home at the same time.'

'He can't write travel books,' Claire said. 'Not good ones. They are too vague. Why don't you go on his travels with him if he just wants to travel?'

Marigold left. It was amazing how very sour she had

turned out to be. Neither Claire nor Tom could understand her.

True enough, that day he had been lunching with Ruth. Claire had simply asked him if he had.

'How did you guess?' he said.

'I have heard,' said Claire, 'that insurance companies move their door-to-door salesmen into areas where redundant workers live, hoping to profit by their lump-sum severance pay.'

It didn't take Tom long to make the analogy between himself and the insurance men, and he protested: 'But we have had to reduce the cast from eleven to seven.'

'How many men?' said Claire.

'Three.'

'Are they married?'

'Two are married. The wives are very boring. One of the actors we laid off is Jonathan Slaker and the other is Wolfgang Hertz. Mrs. Slaker is not young and Mrs. Hertz is a terrifying young computer-accountant. Not my types. Besides, you exaggerate. I'm perfectly happy at home. What about Charlie?'

'Charlie?' she said, for a moment genuinely puzzled.

'Yes, Charlie.'

'Oh Charlie. He's a thing of the past.'

'Redundant,' said Tom.

'You might put it that way,' said Claire.

Tom often wondered if we were all characters in one of God's dreams. To an unbeliever this would have meant the casting of an insubstantiality within an already insubstantial context. Tom was a believer. He meant the very opposite. Our dreams, yes, are insubstantial; the dreams of God, no. They are real, frighteningly real. They bulge with flesh, they drip with blood. My own dreams, said Tom to himself, are shadows, my arguments – all shadows.

Tom started going out at night in a taxi the driver of which he had befriended. All Tom wanted was locomotion. They cruised merely, surprising many participators of the night street drama. Dave, the driver, of second-generation West Indian origin, was in full sympathetic understanding with Tom. He didn't know why Tom wanted to float around the night-life districts without a reference to sex, but since he was a biblically religious married man he deeply enjoyed Tom's religious reflections on such occasions.

'Are you married?' Tom had asked him.

'Yes, my wife's part-time at Harrods in hosiery. We've got three children, a boy of sixteen and two girls, fourteen and eight.'

The taxi with its sign of 'engaged' was waiting at the door in the fading light.

Tom manoeuvred himself down the front door steps with marvellous agility. Claire watched from the dining room window as Tom got in beside the driver and slammed the door shut.

Let us go then, you and I, . . .

'Your wife doesn't mind you going off like this?'

'No, she doesn't mind at all. She knows I like locomotion.'

'My wife would mind,' said Dave.

'Maybe she'd have reason. Claire doesn't interfere.

[64]

Everything I do is basically connected with my work,' Tom said. 'Everything.'

'Claire is rich, a millionaire, I read about her in a magazine,' said Dave. 'American biscuits. She was born into that fabulous family, what's their name? . . .'

Tom had never read any reference to Claire during all the years he had known her, which did not qualify her in terms of her wealth, as if that were her one salient feature. She did not resent the image. In fact she spent some hours of nearly every week-day with two old-fashioned leather-bound ledgers which recorded her charitable transactions; these were then transferred to a computer and rapidly conveyed by her efficient secretary to one of her money-lawyers to deal with. Claire took seriously all letters asking for money, being very clever at discriminating between fraudulent attempts at rip-off and genuine appeals. To this extent alone she submitted without resentment to the idea that she was essentially a money person.

Although it was true that money was a built-in part of Claire's personality, she was many things besides. Tom was fully aware of this. What steadily drew him towards her was her loyalty to him which always predominated over her infidelities; the latter hardly counted. So that, when from time to time Tom muttered to himself or to one of his women friends, 'My wife has a man,' the remark held no foreboding, and no more than a touch of impatience.

Cruising around in those bright-lit streets Tom sat beside his driver, seldom commenting on their surroundings. Faces looked into the windows at the traffic lights, perhaps wondering what they had to buy or sell, sex, drugs, whatever; but on the whole they merged, ignored, with the rest of the traffic.

'It says in the Bible,' said Dave, '"A woman, if she maintain her husband, is full of anger, impudence, and much reproach."'

'Where does that come, in the Bible?'

'Ecclesiastes.'

'The Bible doesn't teach Christian beliefs. It only illustrates them. The Bible came before Christianity by hundreds of years. That's history.'

'Is that really so? I don't believe it.'

'Please yourself. My wife Claire would never reproach me even if she had to maintain me, which she doesn't.'

They were held up in the traffic beside a bright-lit electronics emporium, packed with customers, mostly very young and not very prosperous-looking.

'The less money they have,' said Tom, 'the more home movie-cameras they buy. I don't understand why.'

'They'll put you out of business,' said Dave.

'They look unemployed to me,' said Tom.

'Publicans and sinners.'

'How do you know? No man has hired them. It's in the Bible that Jesus saw those men idle in the market place, looking for jobs. He said they should get paid just the same as those who had work. They were waiting around all day to be hired, and at the end of the day they said "No man has hired us." According to Jesus, they were entitled to their pay just the same as those who had done a day's work.'

'My brother-in-law is out of work,' Dave said. 'He

was in a pizza-bar and they sacked him to take on a man for less pay. He's fighting a case, but in the meantime where does it get him? And he spends more time looking for a job, going through all the regular routes, than a lot of employed fellows. Redundancy worries me; it hangs over us all.'

'There should always be a job for a driver, especially a cab-driver.'

'Should be. But it doesn't work that way.'

Let us go then, you and I, . . .

'Do you know the lines from a poet, T.S. Eliot:

'Let us go then, you and I,
When the evening is spread out against the sky
Like a patient etherised upon a table; . . .'?

'No, never heard that before.'

'What do you suppose it means?'

'Say it again.'

Tom repeated it.

'I'd say it means that here's these people going out for a walk in the evening and they're going to discuss a third person, someone not there. And these two are going to talk about that third person, the patient.'

'Analyse him, take him to bits?'

'Something of that. Don't you know what it means?'

'Nobody really knows.'

When he got home Tom woke up Claire who had just fallen asleep. He handed out his spectacles case to her. 'Imagine,' he said, 'that this contains a present. Show me how you would take it.'

Claire hesitated, smiled, put out her hand and took the case.

'That's it!' said Tom. 'There is a way of accepting a present. The hand should linger. It's been worrying me all day. The actress who's playing Nora snatches it as if the present were going to be taken away from her. But you've got it right, Claire. The hand should linger. It's been nagging me all day. Now, do it again, let's see . . .'

'My niece might well drop out of the film,' said Mrs. Woodstock to young Alec, the top dress designer at Blue Moon's. 'She says he has been simply terrible since he recovered from his accident. He was always a temperamental swine but now he's insufferable. Rose might quit, any day, any hour. Don't be surprised if you hear.'

'The way to get things done, making scenes is definitely not,' Alec remarked as he stood back from Elena Woodstock to observe the effect of some pins he had put into her dress. He came back to her and shifted two pins under her arms. 'He has a reputation,' Alec said, putting his head first to one side and then to another.

'Rose will quit,' said her aunt. 'Do you know what a demand he made on her yesterday? – She had to re-do an action that involved receiving a present from a lover. Well, Rose played it eager. She snatched the jewel case and snapped it open, as she told me, with a kind of gasp. Was that good enough for Tom Richards? No, it wasn't. "You must linger," he said, as if she hasn't been acting these lover-parts for three, four years. "Let the hand *linger*. Don't grab." Well, Rose wasn't grabbing, she was just showing eager to see what jewel her lover had brought. And Tom said in front of everyone, "Rose, I have to talk to you. Tonight, before you go home. I'd like you to have a drink with me as I've something to explain."

'Rose said, "The hell you have, Tom. You can explain why you're picking on me like this. And you don't explain tonight because I have a prior engagement." The truth is, Alec, he's madly in love with Rose and he's so frustrated he screams. Well, yes he started to yell but Rose just left the set. If he doesn't calm down to-day she'll quit the movie. Do you blame her?'

'I don't blame,' said Alec. 'But you know how it is.'

'Rose is so right for the part,' said Mrs. Woodstock.

'Oh, she's ravishing,' said the dressmaker.

CHAPTER EIGHT

It is time now to describe what Tom looked like, six months after his accident, about the time when he completely lost his head over Rose Woodstock, that actress who defied him about how to accept an important present in a film.

The fall had damaged Tom's appearance but by no means ruined it. He was tall with good, even features, wide-spaced long-shaped dark eyes surrounded by some humorous wrinkles. Since his fall he had grown a grisly grey and black beard.

Although it was often said that Tom had survived his fall by a miracle, several realities had in fact contributed towards the accident being less drastic than it might have been. The crane, for instance, was not at its full height but was at that moment being lowered and the seat was possibly at no more than eight feet when Tom fell; the tilt, moreover, pitched Tom on his side rather than his back, and saved his head; he fell into a pile of packing-cases – actually empty – in a scene depicting the back store of a hair-dressing salon, indeed narrowly missing an arrangement of mirrors which would have given him trouble, or killed him, had he crashed upon them. One way and another Tom had been lucky. All his ribs on his right side broken, his right hip badly fractured and the shock had taken up six months of his life. He still walked with a stick. He was as attractive as ever; that is to say, very attractive and at the age of sixty-three his passion for Rose Woodstock, a young thirty-eight, was in no way out of place because of the discrepancy in their ages. He wanted her to be a first-class actress and was furious because he knew she could never be in the first class. She was a star, which was something different. She drove him mad with her opinions of contempt for 'elitism' by which she attempted to rationalise her own professional deficiencies. Tom only wanted to sleep with her successfully.

But he now made love too fast. He could not keep it going. Rose complained, without embarrassment on her side, or the slightest delicacy, that he made love like he was in a hurry to get home. Tom thought of the hamburger girl cooking on the campsite. How tender, how charmingly French and patient she would have been. Rose had wanted to be cast as the hamburger girl but she was not right for that part; which in any case was a comparatively small one. Trained by an academy of dramatic art, Rose was an academy actress from start to finish. Extremely competent, extremely 'Academy'. Any well-informed member of the audience could detect the source of her training. She lifted a glass off the table the 'Academy' way; she received bad news in the 'Academy' style. She was nothing like the hamburger girl of Tom's original conception.

The title of the movie had recently arrived at *A Near Miss* which Tom secretly felt just about described Rose Woodstock's performance. (But in any case, the Gay movement, deeply misunderstanding the meaning of this title when it was announced, had protested, so that the title had been withdrawn and several new suggestions for the title were already being noised about.) Tom's passion for Rose increased as her acting got worse. The cast were losing spontaneity with so many rows and arguments between the director and the star; her performance deteriorated ever more in proportion to the limited time in which Tom was able to maintain a workable erection when he went to bed with her. She complained, too, about his prickly beard ruining her complexion. He took this seriously because of the film; she was gorgeously photogenic.

Claire never waited up for him. Why not? he wondered in his fury, and there and then, at five-thirty in the morning, several times rang up his daughter Marigold to cover her with insults about her flat-chested puritanism and jibes about her husband's extra-marital evasions of duty.

'Pa, I'm writing a book. I went to bed late and you woke me up,' said Marigold.

'What's the book about? The abominations of sexual marriage?'

'It's called *Redundancy and the Self-Employed*.' She added, 'That basically means people like you, Pa. And while we're on personal subjects, your nose is far too long, it sticks out. If I were an artist painting your portrait I'd make it look like a late-comer at a party compared with and joining the rest of your features. Small breasts are very good under clothes.'

'Sometimes,' he said, 'you sound quite intelligent and almost human. I don't say you are so but you sound so. And only sometimes. You need a man to wake you up, and that's the truth, Marigold.'

Tom no longer needed his nurse. Twice a week for three-quarters of an hour, he succumbed to a physio-therapist who took him through his exercises. The Greek masseur, Ron, came every Saturday afternoon. Tom missed his crew of attendants and confidants. Their personal histories which he had become acquainted with were now lost to him forever like tele-vision serials broken off and never resumed. The last of the nurses to go was Tom's day nurse Julia. He had got used to the developing stories of her three children and her husband. Julia herself had another job to go to but her husband, second mechanic in a garage, whose job had seemed so safe, was made redundant the week before her job with Tom came to an end. He had asked her to keep in touch, let him know how the family were doing. He never heard.

He felt that all through his illness from the accident and convalescence, he had been directing a film, inter-viewing interminable faces for casting with a mixture of critical scrutiny, cynicism and sincere involvement which, to him, represented sixty per cent of a film. It was a surrealistic process, this casting and creatively feeling at the same time. At the initial stages faces and shapes affected the form of his movies much more than the screenplay itself. Until a film was three-quarters completed, when people asked him what the film was 'about', he simply laughed in their faces.

Tom mused: 'I fell off my perch. Now I want a divorce from my past ideas. How do I achieve this?'

Let us go then, you and I, . . .

Dave the taxi-driver, expensive but true friend that he was, sat in the driver's seat negotiating the traffic. Tom sat beside him, so rich as he was, so democratic. 'What you never say,' Dave remarked, 'is what your film's about.'

Tom laughed.

'Why laugh? It's a question. You talk about your film, this image, that impression, so on, so on. You cut, you save and you scrap. But what's it about?'

'A girl,' said Tom. 'A girl I saw one day on a campsite in France. I stopped for a coffee at a stall on the edge of the camp. A girl was making hamburgers. She was nothing much, just a girl. But I saw her in a frame. When I see people in frames I know I want to make a film of just that picture.'

'Pictures inside frames,' said Dave.

'That's really all there is to it,' said Tom. 'The title of the movie is at present *The Lump Sum . . .*'

The Lump Sum . . . Tom knew that his film would not end up with that title. But how he longed in his wish-dream to settle a lump sum on that young, poor hamburger woman. To do it in an anonymous way so that she never knew how or why this fortune had come to her. It would have to be untraceable. What would be the consequence to her?

She could be initially shocked, incredulous, then gradually indifferent, accepting her vast fortune (artistically, it would have to be immense) with indifference as to its source. Once assured it was really hers, all hers, she could possibly slip into the part without difficulty, settling her family and friends, escaping from them (paying off her husband if she had one), starting a new life.

Or, she could be forever curious, never at ease. She could possibly start a search, so that the anonymous benefactor was the subject of a long pursuit; he would be perpetually in flight, always very nearly caught, but not quite. (Until, perhaps, the end.) The hamburger girl could employ the most expensive detectives, a computerised network of clue-hunters, infallible, international. How does one give away a virtual financial empire (it had to be an empire) without detection? Tom was seized with nostalgia for that hospital-dream of his when, under the influence of drugs and injections, he had thought calmly of murdering Claire so that he could inherit her money and settle it on the hamburger girl. (But even then he had known that Claire's considerable fortune was not enough, artistically.)

Suppose he should now say to his wife: 'Claire, I need X millions to give away to a girl as an experiment,' what would she do? It would be like her answer to his request for the Sèvres dinner plates in order to break them in a mood of exasperation. She had sent to his room a pile of plates from the supermarket, absolutely useless for his purpose. It would be like that. Instead of X millions for his experiment Claire would, perhaps, suggest a few, some X hundreds; interesting, but another story altogether, a mere kindly act, not at all to the point. What he needed was all Claire's millions, every last million.

Now the hamburger girl of his dreams would naturally mistake the motive of the donor. She would imagine that her personal attractions were what the anonymous multi-millionaire had 'taken a fancy' to. She would probably look at herself in the mirror and see a beauty, whereas she was not a beauty, only a fairly presentable slim young girl cooking hamburgers. Would she tell all her friends? Or only some of her friends? The fiscal problem – would capital gains come into it? The legal question, all to be settled, her great fears allayed. The hamburger girl might feel she would one day have to pay in some sexual terms and might come to a near-breakdown deciding whether to give up the fortune or fight the case – but what 'case'?

She might become very stingy, a miser, imagining that everyone was after her money. Everyone might well be after her money, especially her family, her men friends. The girl on the campsite wore no wedding ring. She did not appear to be a married girl. She might, with enormous wealth, make a good social marriage. She could find a *bon parti* who would arrange for her to have driving lessons and learn to speak English (for she was still a French girl on that campsite). She could afford to pay off endless fortune-hunters till she found the right one, if ever.

'Do you think,' said Tom to Dave, 'that she would know what to do with that sort of money? Would she ever learn?'

'It depends on the girl,' Dave said. 'It seems to me

you've forgotten that the girl has a character, a personality, already functioning before you saw her dishing
out hamburgers. She was already a person. It depends
on her what she would do.'

'The charm of this girl is that she has no history,'
Tom said.

'Then she isn't real.'

'No, she's not real. Not yet.'

Like a patient etherised upon a table; . . .

Rose Woodstock, the actress who had been persuaded
in the film to play the part of the rich and eccentric
benefactor's girl-friend, had not improved, not greatly,
in the act of receiving a present. Tom accepted the last
few pictures of her taking and opening a box containing
a necklace. Her hand did tremble a little more than it
had done at first, but Tom saw that this was as far as
he could get with her. As a practised director he knew
when he could go no further with his demands on an
actor. It was in any case enough that Rose looked plaus-
ible. She was a star without great quality.

She was a box-office draw, written into the film for
that reason.

The hamburger girl herself was essentially a minor
personality. The actress's name was Jeanne both in the
movie and in the flesh. The whole point of the movie
was that the hamburger girl should not be a star. Jeanne
should be a throw-away item seen always at an angle.

Well, Tom told himself that it was enough. But in
fact nothing was enough. The film had been held up
by his accident. It had been stopped; it had been

shelved; then unshelved, as he recovered in health, dusted off and started again. Now that it was once more in progress, the difference was that now he was in love with the overwhelming beauty Rose Woodstock, a fact which discouraged that very attractive waif-like nonentity Jeanne who played so well that subordinate role, the hamburger girl. Jeanne, with her high cheekbones and ragged hairstyle, was not only discouraged by Tom's indifference to her off the set; she was positively infuriated. She knew she was essentially the important personality of the film. Jeanne resented the glow of attention that Tom turned on box-office Rose whenever she appeared on or off the set.

Rose had counted on the screenplay being altered so that her status was no longer mistress; when the benefactor made love to her in bed, at intervals in the film, with much heaving and munching, he 'saw' the hamburger girl.

Rose Woodstock's husband in real life was a young television director, at present without work. Tom paid him for a while. Tom imagined that Rose was not supposed to know about this, but she did. As the shooting of the film proceeded she fell commercially but genuinely in love with Tom, which in her case was possible.

The producers now wanted to make Jeanne into a more prominent personality. Tom's financial share in the film, together with his reputation, gave him a good say on the artistic side.

They called a meeting. It took place in a beige suite at the top of a London hotel. Five people in all, two of whom, a man and a woman, were silent.

'Jeanne is nothing. Nothing at all. She's a throw-away

item. You see her only at an angle. She's an idea. If you make her a somebody,' Tom said, 'the movie falls to pieces. It is nothing. Nothing at all.'

He compromised by agreeing to do more close-ups of Jeanne. 'I'll have to look at Rose's contract. She'll be furious. I'll have to work in a few more close-ups of Rose.'

'Close-ups of Rose are always money in the bank,' observed one member of the meeting, philosophically.

Tom cruised around with Dave that night. 'The trouble with producers,' Tom said, 'they want both an art film and a commercial success. They want sentimentality, emotion and the higher moods of detachment. They want bloody everything. Fortunately I have some money of my own in the film which gives me a certain pull. But I'm both director and script-writer which means I have to appear to hear everybody's ideas while taking no notice of them.'

'Follow your instinct,' Dave advised. 'Ignore the rest.'

'But I'm in love with Rose,' said Tom. 'So much in love, I can't tell you. Off the set she is simply delicious.'

'Sounds unprofessional.'

'Oh, it's not professional,' Tom said. 'But the greatest trouble is Jeanne. She suspects I'm having an affair with Rose. She resents what seems to be her minor role in the film when she is in fact the important element in it. The whole environment of the movie world is bad for Jeanne's acting. She is beginning to get ideas.'

Not long after this Jeanne phoned Tom's house at about nine at night. As she had imagined Tom wasn't in. 'Could I speak to Mrs. Richards?'

'I'm Jeanne, the hamburger girl,' said Jeanne.

'Oh, hello, Jeanne. My husband's not here. He's probably still in the studio, in the projection-room or at a rehearsal.'

'Oh, no, he isn't in the studio,' said Jeanne. 'Oh, no, he is not.'

'Well perhaps he's in conference, in which case he'll be home late. Can I give him a message?'

'No,' said Jeanne. 'But I can tell you where Tom is, Mrs. Richards. He's in Rose Woodstock's London flat. Her husband's in the country.'

'In that case why do you ring him up here? I daresay they're discussing the film – but why don't you call him there?' said Claire. 'That's to say if you have the number. I'm afraid I don't have it. But if there's anything urgent I'll leave Tom a message. He'll get it first thing.'

'First thing in the morning, Mrs. Richards?'

'That could be,' said Claire. 'But you know, Tom might be back any time, any minute. He's still under therapy and has to go carefully . . .'

'He's in love with Rose Woodstock. Don't you realise?' Jeanne said. She sounded tired, exasperated.

'Oh, no, that's not at all the case,' said Claire. 'He thinks of nobody but you, Jeanne. Don't you see how it is? He talks day and night about his hamburger girl. The original he saw on a campsite in France. I was there at the time. He's obsessed by you, Jeanne.'

'He treats me so badly,' said Jeanne. She had started to cry. She seemed to have quite forgotten that she was talking to a wife. Claire continued to extend sympathy. She was expansive. She finally got Jeanne off the phone somehow. Then she scribbled a note to Tom: 'Jeanne is *looking* for you' and left this on the hall table. Then she put on her television glasses and went back to her programme.

CHAPTER NINE

'My father suggested I should interview you,' said Marigold. 'As I said, I'm writing a book on redundancy. Could you tell me some of your experiences as a redundant T.V. programme director. What were your first feelings when you were told to go?'

'You can't imagine,' said Kevin Woodstock.

'Oh yes I can,' said Marigold. 'I am a redundant wife. I was told. Just like that.'

'I was stunned.' Rain splashed at the small windows of Marigold's cottage in Surrey.

'Me, too. After a while I realised that I expected it. But at the first moment I was stunned,' Marigold told him.

'Yes, I should have expected it, too. I had programmes planned ahead. They had to be scrapped. Crow Television paid out, all round. I got offered a lump sum but my lawyer's fighting it.'

'Were you the only one made redundant?'

'No, seven of us had to go.' He gulped his beer. Marigold sipped her calorie-free Coke.

'Have you thought of emigrating?' Marigold said.

'Yes,' he said. 'But where to? My wife is in demand for motion pictures all the time in the U.K. and the U.S. There's nothing for me abroad. Rose would never emigrate even if so.'

'Have you thought of T.V. ads? Commercials?'

'Rose wouldn't like that. It would be a come-down. It would affect her career as an actor (she won't be called actress, by the way) if I went on the T.V. pushing track-shoes, mountain bikes, holiday homes, whatever.'

'Has your redundancy affected your matrimonial life?'

'There's a danger of that,' said Kevin Woodstock, 'but don't quote me personally on the question.' For some inscrutable reason he added, 'We've been married eleven years. Rose uses her married name professionally.'

Marigold assured him he was, for her purpose, an anonymous case history.

She had thought him charming but she had made up her mind not to be personally influenced by any such fact. However, when he said, 'I hope that you, as a redundant wife, will be free for dinner,' she accepted.

Although they left Surrey in Marigold's car, because of the problems of parking Marigold drove it to her private garage in her small mews flat off Brompton Road, where she left it. They then got a taxi to Soho to an Indian restaurant called Dish Delhi, arriving about nine o'clock. They left shortly after eleven-thirty. Marigold took a taxi home. He walked a short distance until a cruising taxi passed which he took to his home at Camden Town.

It was towards the end of September, when Tom's film had been finished and was off his hands for the past three weeks, that Tom said to Claire, 'Have you seen Marigold lately?'

She had not. Nobody else they knew had seen or heard of Marigold for many weeks. This was not so very unusual, but the length of time during which she did not ring or show up, was beginning to be unusual. She didn't answer the phone. Her cleaning woman had gone to Spain for her holidays and being unable to get into the mews flat on her return, presumed Marigold to have gone off somewhere. Her daily help in her cottage in Surrey had not seen her.

One way and another it was now almost five weeks that Marigold was missing.

Marigold was the one settled thing in common between Claire and Tom. She kept telling her parents that they had nothing in common, and therefore should divorce, not realising that she – that the appalling nature of their only offspring – was mainly the cause of Claire and Tom's inseparability. They were drawn together in wondering about Marigold and guilt about their feelings towards her. Even her disagreeable face kept them together like birds in a storm.

Marigold had made a home-movie video cassette on the subject of redundancy. In a simulated job-interview she played the part of the prospective employer. This she sent to Tom 'for his information' meaning for his approval. He watched it with Claire and found it terribly funny. Marigold's face on the screen came out in this very amateur production bloated, blotched with too many depressive turn-down lines. Her eyes had faded somehow. (Wasn't she, surely, an addict or ex-addict of something?) Tom and Claire hurled themselves about the sofa in their hilarity. Marigold's voice croaked authoritatively, nastily:

'On what grounds were you made redundant? Was it a group action? Was it individual performance?'

The idiotic actor being interviewed, nervously touched his tie and said, from the dreadful, prepared script, 'It was actually the latter criterion which applied in my case.'

'That is a mark against you,' Marigold said, her face twitching. 'One mark at least.'

They switched it off before the end. Tom took the cassette out of the machine. 'My God,' he said, 'however did we spawn her?'

Claire was literally dabbing the corner of her eyes, still convulsed with laughter.

This had been roughly three weeks from the night Marigold was last seen by Kevin Woodstock in the taxi that bore her from the restaurant.

Tom had put the cassette aside, mentally composing in his mind a tactful note to Marigold, or a way of approach if she should turn up confronting him for an opinion, 'Marigold, I could have it done professionally for you. There is just a touch of the amateur. Of course, I understand that this is intended for job-consultants, yes, yes, I quite understand . . .'

The cassette lay on one side where he had put it. Later, finding it, he handed it to Claire. They were now childless and clouded over with guilt.

Claire remembered one of the last times she had seen Marigold, who had kept on bitching about Tom's affair with Rose and what she called his shabby treatment of Jeanne. Marigold had taken the trouble to inform herself about the gossip flying around the studio where *The Hamburger Girl* (again the title) was winding to an end.

'Your pride. How can you stand it?' Marigold said. 'You must feel terrible.'

'And how do you feel about being abandoned?' said Claire.

'It's a totally different case,' screamed Marigold. 'A mother shouldn't talk to a daughter like that.'

Hideous Marigold. Always negative Marigold. Her parents had searched through the past, consulted psychiatrists, took every moment to bits. In no way could she be explained. The second psychiatrist had even interviewed Marigold. 'You see,' he told Claire, 'it's a cocktail. Personality is a mixture of genes. You can't do anything about it. You can't put there what there isn't a place for, you can't take anything away without leaving a bad trace. She would have to want to change.'

'She won't do that,' said Tom, 'not her.'

He always thought secretly of Cora, the loving and the beautiful. Claire, too, was attached to Cora. In her way Marigold got on quite well with her older half-sister. She had never showed signs of jealousy. Marigold had been jealous of no-one, in fact. She was too satisfied with herself for envy, jealousy or the like.

'If it had been Cora, I think I'd feel less appalled,' Tom said to Claire soon after Marigold's disappearance, trying to cope with it as they were.

'I'd feel the same,' Claire said. 'With Marigold, there's

a feeling of frustration, of unfinished business. I think of her face, the tragic mask. Why?'

'That's it,' Tom said. 'You've said it exactly. It's unfinished business.'

Whether it was an unconscious memory of these words or not, Tom had the title of his film changed the next week, finally, to *Unfinished Business*. He hardly knew he had done so. He busied himself unnecessarily in perfecting the film; he dropped Rose Woodstock as a lover. But concentrated on her, on Jeanne, and on the actor who had played his part in the video on redundancy, only as possible accomplices in the disappearance of Marigold. Had she been murdered? In fact, his feelings were chaotic.

'The century is old,' said Tom in one of his more lucid moments with Claire; 'it is very old.'

CHAPTER TEN

The answers that Marigold's family and friends were able to give to the police about her habits, her possible movements, her whereabouts, only served to show how little anyone knew her. Tom's indignant guilt sent the investigators on grotesquely false trails. He was not convinced she had been abducted and killed, as was certainly held by the police to be a strong possibility. Claire clung to the theory that Marigold had just wandered or walked off the scene, possibly to start a new life. It was impossible to know if she had taken money or precious objects, maybe jewellery, with her. Nobody knew about her money, her goods. It appeared just then that Marigold had been all her life exceedingly secretive.

Cora said: 'I feel we should have taken more interest in Marigold.'

'So do I,' said Tom. 'But how? How?'

Tom thought back on the times he had tried to make Marigold part of the family. Her manners were frightful. She was a positive embarrassment at any party that involved her parents' friends. This was apparent before her fifteenth year, when she could be described as 'difficult'. But as her adolescence wore off, she became ever more aggressive, ever more impossible to have around the house, ever less welcome in a house where some elements of domestic staff were necessary. Tom and Claire tended at first to blame themselves. But they were in no wise to blame. Marigold was simply a natural disaster.

Her marriage had been a touch and go affair. Her property – the house in Surrey and the flat in London – together with her very wealthy mother, made her into a material catch. But it could never have lasted.

Discussing her one day as they often did, Claire said to Tom, 'Another thing I don't understand about Marigold – she can be so *common*. Where does she get that vulgarity? From which of us, from what side, does the street-corner touch come?'

Nobody could answer that one.

Tom told the police investigators who enquired about her character, 'I know very little about that. She resembles neither my wife nor me, except that, like me, she's sexy.'

'Do you mean she might have gone off with anybody?'

'Yes, she might, if she fancied the man. Or the woman.'

'Any idea what she might be doing for money?'

'No, we don't know anything about where she keeps her money. She had plenty from her mother. It might be deposited all over the place, just anywhere.'

The police investigator was in plain clothes. A grey suit, a grey tie. Tom would not have cast him as a policeman. He thought the face too soft, too much the face of a man who resembled his mother rather than his father. And yet, Tom reflected, perhaps, after all, this would be the ideal casting. Not at all the *cliché* of a police officer. Yes, he would be interesting in the part. (But what part?)

'Have you faced the possibility that she might be dead?' the policeman asked.

'You mean murdered?'

'Yes.'

'I am not convinced about that. In fact, I haven't thought on those lines,' said Tom. 'Should I?'

'It's one of the possibilities,' said the man.

'And you're working on that possibility?'

'Oh, yes.'

'She could walk in at any time,' Tom said. 'Just any time. She must know the worry she's causing.'

The papers had been full of Marigold's disappearance, especially when she was first definitely missed.

'But,' Tom added, 'I'm not sure that she'd care about us, how we feel. In a way that fact is a hopeful sign.'

Tom was in fact thinking the deeply disloyal thought 'Why should anyone *bother* to murder Marigold?'

'It may be,' he said to the officer, 'she has just gone away to write a novel.'

'Has she expressed a desire to that effect?'

'No. But everyone is writing a novel, why not Marigold?'

'You feel she's alive somewhere?'

'I have a hunch that she is, that's all.'

'Try,' said the policeman, 'to analyse your hunch. If you come up with anything, any clue, let us know. We ourselves have no hunches.'

They had been through Marigold's diary, and had interviewed nineteen people who had been interviewed by Marigold in connection with her research on redundancy.

'You say she seemed an eccentric.'

'I didn't say that. I said she was a strange sort of woman.'

'Attractive?'

'Not really. But all right in bed for a few hours.'

'Why did you have sex with her?'

'She invited me. She was out with it – just like that. No mimble-mamble.'

'Why did you accept?'

'I felt it was part of the interview, and I felt inclined. When you've lost your job you need something to make you feel good.'

Another man explained, 'I knew she was the daughter of Tom Richards, the film director. A name is a glamorous lay, isn't it?'

One of the women the police interviewed gave the information: 'She was very eager to know how much I spent on my clothes and beauty products, and how much I needed those items to keep a job.'

'Didn't you think it was a normal question for someone studying the economics of employment and unemployment?'

'Yes, but she went on about it.'

'Did she suggest to you a lesbian relationship?'

'No, she didn't. She wanted to know about the men,

always the men, in my office where I had been working. Did "redundant" mean only that one wouldn't sleep with them, and so on.'

'And did redundancy mean that in your case?'

'No, it didn't. It just meant that eight of us lost our jobs.'

'She didn't use her married name, apparently. Would you say that Marigold Richards disliked, resented, men?'

'Perhaps, a bit. She didn't look as if she could hold a man. But she was interested, more, in sex. I was rather embarrassed by her questions. Don't think I'm inhibited by sex –'

'Neither am I,' said the police officer. 'Without sex none of us would be here. But we're trying to find a woman who's vanished, and some sort of motive . . .'

Cora gave out the possibility that Johnny, her nearly ex-husband, might have induced Marigold to join him in India where she presumed he still was in his flight from materialism.

'Why should he do that?'

'He was in a phase of rejecting conventional ideas of beauty,' Cora said.

The policeman looked at good-looking Cora in amazement. 'We'll follow that line,' he said. They did not need to follow it very far. Handsome Johnny Carr had returned from India and was consoling Rose Wood-stock in Tom's absence.

Tom confided to the taxi-driver Dave as they cruised the night-lit streets: 'Marigold,' he said, 'is a wrecker.

But in a way I'm closer to my wife, Claire, than I've been since we were young. Claire feels badly: her only child. At least I have Cora. And I can't help saying to myself, thank God Cora is safe.'

'Do you mean that Marigold's a wrecker or that she's a victim – which?' said Dave.

'I don't think anything,' Tom said. 'But I can't cast Marigold in the role of victim.'

'Some people suspect you,' said Dave.

'I know. I can feel it in the air. Why should I want to do away with Marigold, I'd like to know?'

'Blackmail, they say. They say she knew too much.'

'Too much about what?'

'About you and Rose Woodstock and the little actress Jeanne somebody.'

'I have no secrets of that kind. Jeanne is a wasp. I've actually dropped Rose. The worry of it all has put me right off her. And do you know what? – She's left her husband entirely and has moved in with Cora's husband Johnny.'

'I saw them, yes, in a magazine. They look a good-looking couple.'

'What feelings can she have, with her husband out of work?'

'He was already out of work when she was with you.'

'Thanks for reminding me. He was the last person we know of to see Marigold. She taped a sample interview with him for her study of redundancy. They had dinner together. Then – then nothing. No bed, no sex. Apparently the subject didn't arise; do you believe it? Nothing. The rest is silence. And where are my friends? Where are they?'

[94]

'Are you sure,' said Dave, 'you aren't imagining things? Not everyone is gossiping about you. They don't all believe in rumours. Far from it.'

After a while Dave added, 'In any case maybe the truth is that she left of her own free-will to make a break from you. Your name alone is overpowering. Think of it.'

The press had made much of the 'relations' between Marigold and Tom.

'All my so-called friends have talked to the press. In the old days,' Tom said, 'there would have been plenty of friends stop by to see me after all the fuss and talk in the press, on the T.V. They would have called me up from wherever they were. Now all they can do is make publicity for themselves by giving interviews. "Marigold as I knew her," "Marigold has something to fear," "Has she lost her memory?" So on, so on. If Binkie Beaumont was still alive he would have rung me, asked me round for a drink. He was a powerful theatre producer, Tennent's. The world's biggest queer but very abounding in hospitality there in Lord North Street. He was convinced his house had been a brothel to serve the Houses of Parliament. There were little wash-basins in some of the rooms, which Binkie just left there, and also some parliamentary division bells had been installed. So I suppose he was right. It was a brothel or the house of someone's mistress. There one met *tout le monde*. But Binkie was afraid of death. He didn't like the subject or even the word. This sometimes limited his choice of plays. All the same, Binkie would have called me up to show solidarity. But Binkie's dead. Essentially, Dave, a person consists of memories.'

'Are we born with memories?' Dave said.

'There is a theory of that nature. It well might be.'

'I just wondered. Sometimes I seem to know of things I couldn't possibly have experienced. And sometimes the children come out with something that makes you wonder: Wherever did they pick that up from? As if they knew things from a time before they were born.'

'Children are quite psychic,' Tom said. 'Very intuitive. They can tune into your thoughts, it's a bit disquieting. You should try always to give them happy memories. It's the only thing you can leave to your children with any certainty – happy memories.'

'I lost a lot of friends,' said Dave. 'And now they've gone, they're only memories. And I missed the chance of talking to them about a great number of subjects. In my trade one meets people. Now it's too late.'

'Don't you make new friends?' Tom said.

'No, I don't seem to, Tom. You excepted. The people who get in a taxi, even the regulars, don't talk. They sit back and close in with themselves.'

Tom, also, was now closed in with himself. He was thinking how afraid everyone was since Marigold's disappearance, to get mixed up with him. Just in case . . . Tennessee Williams, he thought, would have called me from the States. He often called on the phone, often and often. He would have been a true friend. Tom remembered the last time he met Tennessee, at a party in New York in the sixties, at Edward Albee's place. The party was given for the Russian Ballet but they didn't turn up. Not allowed. Noël Coward, still then very much alive, had slithered over to him with that walk of his, 'Can you *really* understand Albee's plays?'

he had asked Tom, almost within ear-shot of his host. Tom had replied, 'I'm fascinated by Albee, in fact.' 'Are you really, darling?'

Tom said to Dave, 'Auden would have asked me to dinner without mentioning Marigold. He would have gone out of his way to do so. The last time I saw Auden was in his house at Kirchstetten outside Vienna. I found Wystan going through different editions of Agatha Christie, marking them up at the places where she deleted her colour-racism or softened her anti-semitism over the years. We thought of making a film of Proust. It's almost impossible. There was a film but it was no good. It wasn't Proust. Did you ever read any Proust?'

'No, I haven't,' Dave said.

'Have a try,' said Tom. 'The English translation is better than the original French, many people say. I'll bring you a volume. Auden agreed that Proust's twelve-volume novel was economic compared with Joyce's *Finnegans Wake* or *Ulysses*. He thought Joyce long-winded and ill-mannered towards the public. Auden himself had wonderful manners. Except, of course, when pushed.'

'You should write your memoirs,' Dave said.

'I mean to do so as soon as we have definite news of Marigold. Until then, I can do nothing with my memories except go over the people I've seen more recently, the world I've been living in lately.'

'That's an idea,' Dave said. 'You might hit on a clue to her whereabouts. Memory's a wonderful thing.'

'I'm like a drowning man sometimes,' Tom said. 'The events of my life flash past in my mind. Perhaps I'll remember something useful without any effort.'

'My sympathy to Mrs. Richards,' Dave said.

'I'll tell Claire.'

Claire woke about four every morning with a sudden idea about the whereabouts of Marigold. Had she gone on a climbing trip to Nepal? Had she returned to the cottage in Provence she had once rented for a holiday? Or was she in the Haute Savoie on some campsite pretending to be, or imagining she was, Tom's hamburger girl? Claire would resolve to investigate all the possibilities that occurred to her in the middle of the night, would settle down to sleep restlessly, but in the morning when she woke again she would feel paralysed by the improbability, the futility, of her ideas.

The thought that Marigold might be somewhat out of her mind had taken a hold on Tom. He was convinced that if she was still alive she had lost her memory. When Claire said, one morning, 'In the middle of the night it came to me that Marigold might be looking for your hamburger girl, the real one, perhaps impersonating her. But how could she?'

'Why not?' said Tom. 'Why not? She was always resentful of that dream of mine. She could well have been driven by rancour. Let's go to that campsite and see.'

It was the end of September. 'Let's see,' Tom said. In his film the campsite had been located in Scotland. It had required very few shots. In the film Jeanne had stood over her makeshift stove stolidly making hamburgers. She had only once raised her eyes. That was when she caught sight of the older man looking at her, watching. She had dropped her eyelids again, intent on her hamburgers, dishing them out to the holiday makers as they queued up outside her tiny kiosk.

The campsite in the Haute Savoie was still there, a number of trailers were lined up at the bottom of the field. Jeanne's kiosk was there, shuttered up. The camp itself was closed. At the hotel nearby where they stopped for the night, Tom showed a photograph of Marigold. The owner, at the reception desk shook his head, but his wife, a large woman who stood looking over his shoulder said, 'One moment. Perhaps . . . Recently, I don't know . . . We have so many clients coming and going . . .' They looked up Marigold's names, both married and unmarried, in the register dating back long before Marigold's disappearance. There was no sign of her there.

Nothing was certain. Nothing was resolved. Tom and Claire ate a delicious meal at the hotel; enjoying it in spite of their anxiety.

'Why on earth should we distress ourselves like this?' Tom said. 'What have we done?'

'I, too, am asking myself, What are we doing here?' Claire said.

They ate their good French dinner in rather a better mood, both feeling that by their visit to the campsite they had exhausted their duty. The very fancified menu was translated into an English which they contemplated with some pleasure, the main course being 'steak with an escort of green runner beans and a fanfare of pan-fried red pepper.'

The amusement of Tom and Claire over the wording of the menu was a small matter compared to the hilarity of Marigold and her new lover, shacked up as they were in one of the forlorn trailers on the campsite where her parents had stood surveying the desolate scene.

'They had a hunch I'd be here,' spluttered Marigold, 'and I had a hunch that they'd have that hunch. He's obsessed with his hamburger girl, and there they were standing and looking right at us.'

'Why didn't they look thoroughly? They could easily have found us. Why shouldn't we be here, anyway?'

'They don't want to find me,' Marigold said. She was now smiling her very grim smile. 'That's the truth. Deep down, they don't want me around.'

'What a laugh! To see them standing there . . . Will you let them know?'

'One day, yes.'

They had been three days in the trailer and were

about to leave. Marigold had only partly dreamed that Tom and Claire would follow her to this very spot which she had read about in some of the film's pre-release publicity. The place had been in his mind for over a year. 'The idea came to Tom Richards when he made a casual stop at a campsite . . .' The actual place had been photographed, in the fulness of its high summer activity. Buckets and washing and children's swings. People in shorts. Children everywhere. At the entrance a little kiosk with a girl with her back to the camera serving hamburgers. It was anybody's campsite, but it was near the village Tom had mentioned so often. That had been the reality from which Tom's dream had emerged. The trailers were now empty, detached from their motors. 'Let's wait here,' Marigold had said. 'I'm sure this is the spot. But will he come here looking for me? It's a long, long shot but we could wait and see.'

Her companion made a deal for three days with the trailer's owner, actually a brother of the man who owned the hotel. And on the third day, at five-twenty in the afternoon, look! 'That's my mother and father,' she said, peeping from the window, incredulous.

'What a bitch you are!' said the man. With which observation Marigold seemed well pleased.

The producers of Tom's film worried about the effect of Marigold's disappearance.

The police had moved on to a theory of suicide. Any scenario would fit: that she was depressed by the desertion of her husband to the extent that she had taken herself to the Alps and thrown herself over a precipice;

that she had taken herself out to sea and jumped over-board (but from what boat?); that her body was lying at the bottom of a deep Scottish loch. She was sighted in New Orleans, however, having a good time in a discothèque; she was sighted in a cathedral in Spain, wearing a black mantilla, going to confession; she was 'seen' in New Delhi buying a ruby and diamond brace-let. Interpol got nowhere with these various signals and sightings. It was impossible to say whether the film was affected. Certainly, Tom's personal popularity was low, for, in the meantime, Rose Woodward and Jeanne had grabbed as much publicity as possible out of the burn-ing event, as if with long-handled tongs. Rose admitted her affair with Tom: 'He was fantastically in love with me until the Disappearance. I feel sure Marigold was wounded and sometimes I blame myself. Tom neg-lected his daughter, I know. She wasn't beautiful, she had no glamour. Yes, I know I'm talking in the past tense. I'm well aware of it. But I can't help feeling that Marigold is no longer with us in this world. No, Tom frankly *didn't like* Marigold. She was the first to visit him after his recent accident, when he fell from a crane in the studio – (I was there) – Marigold would have done anything for him. Her mother, Claire, was I think rather cold, for a mother. Poor Marigold, she did what she could to keep her family together. She has a half-sister, Cora. Cora was always the favourite. I don't know – I doubt – if Tom will ever make another film. The original Jeanne, the girl who made hamburgers for a holiday camp, was no longer on his mind when we got together in the course of the film. Jeanne, the little actress who plays the part of the original girl, was really puzzled I think that Tom had no passion for her outside of her professional role about which he was always enthusiastic, of course. But Jeanne as a person – no.

'I think Jeanne had met Marigold, and it could be that Marigold was trying to get her father to take an interest in getting Jeanne another job now that the movie was over. She was out of work. But Tom simply wasn't interested. If he in fact knows where Marigold is, as some of us believe, he should come forward openly. It has made a vital difference to my life as a friend of Tom, indeed to everyone's life. We are all very upset.'

Jeanne's main interview, published in a weekly paper, went: 'As Jeanne, the namesake part I played in the movie, I felt I had at last arrived. It was actually the most important role, and my first big chance. Tom Richards meant everything to me. He was my inspiration and guide. When he had his accident I felt I could never act for anyone else but I was under pressure by Claire, Tom's wife, mainly. She assured me that Tom wanted me to press ahead until he was out and about again. We were told that the movie was off; then it was on again. Well I know he had a family and the girls Cora and Marigold. The other actors in the film didn't greatly interest me although they were terribly kind and very, very competent. I did my best to make a big part of it but somehow Tom's story line treated me like a secondary star and Rose Woodstock as a first even though the story shows a different situation, in fact quite the reverse. All I had to do really in the movie was stand and make hamburgers taken from different shots.

'After this opportunity I want truly to find my feet

in a more important part. I'm out of work, redundant. I actually contacted Marigold as she's a sort of consultant. I think personally that Marigold is still alive. Only she felt, as I felt, Tom Richards' neglect. Now Rose Woodstock is I believe on the margin of his interest as a result of his involvement with Marigold's disappearance. It is a mystery I don't want to be mixed up with, personally.'

In the mail came anonymous letters to Tom either with 'clues' as to Marigold's whereabouts or with accusations: WHAT HAVE YOU DONE WITH MARIGOLD?

All these, Tom passed to the police. His life had changed.

As the weeks passed it was plain that Marigold had not been kidnapped. Various attempts to extort money from Claire on this basis had been easily exposed. 'She's of age. She can come and go as she pleases,' the chief police investigator explained to Tom. 'But we're keeping all possibilities open. We haven't given up.' Tom sensed a touch of impatience with people whose lifestyle permitted the probability that they were not murdered or kidnapped – people who could just walk out of one life into another.

Claire had employed a private investigator: 'Could she, in your opinion, have taken an overdose? Was she on drugs?'

'Oh it's possible,' said Tom. 'They all are.'

'But do you yourself think so?'

'No, I don't. The girl's very puritanical.'

'That's not to say . . .' said the investigator.

'True enough. But you could still find her, couldn't you?'

Marigold's formidable face continued for a while to look out of the pages of the glossy magazines, accompanied by captions such as 'Marigold: Was she a drop-out in the eyes of her glamorous parents?' Inset would be a picture of Claire and Tom, in deck-chairs, looking radiant. Or a picture of gorgeous Cora: 'The sister whose good looks Marigold could never attain.'

'And yet,' Tom said to Claire, 'Marigold could be quite handsome. It isn't her features, it's her expression that's so awful. If she could only get rid of that expression she could have a certain *look*. I don't know what part she could be cast in, but there is a part somewhere for her.'

'The part of a bloody bore,' said Claire.

'Well, in fact, you're right,' he said. 'She is nemesis in drag. She is the Last Judgement. Alive or dead, that's what she is. And in the meantime, I'm getting a bad press. You – and Cora – are also getting a bad press, although you don't deserve it in any way.'

'Neither do you,' said Claire.

'Perhaps I do, but I don't know how,' Tom said. 'I only know the nicest thing that could happen to Marigold, and make her happy, is that we should have a bad reputation on her account. And you know it's true.'

'There's a touch of blackmail involved in her disappearance.'

'More than a touch.'

Claire's investigator, Ivan Simpson, a young, good-looking man not yet thirty, was galvanised by Cora's beauty into volunteering for longer hours than were normally called for in the search for a missing person. He put it to Cora: 'As her sister – well, half-sister – your help would be invaluable. I have a few ideas where we could go, some likely places where she has to be looked for. I'm going to talk about them to your step-mother. Will you help?' Cora said, 'Fine. But if she saw me, wouldn't she go further into hiding?'

'She won't see you. Leave it to me.'

'If she doesn't want to be found maybe she should be left alone . . .'

'Come with me,' he said to the lovely girl. He thought she had the clearest complexion, the clearest eyes and whitest teeth it was possible to imagine. He noticed that her features were perfect, her body charming. She wore brief skirts or tight blue jeans. Her brown hair fell about her shoulders.

He came to Claire who was busy with her charities – her ledgers and lists – and told her his plan. France, the United States: he had clues to follow and he wanted Cora with him.

'And Cora?' said Claire.

'She'll come.'

'Ask her father,' said Claire. 'If Tom's willing, so am I. We'll pay whatever's necessary. If Marigold doesn't want to come back, that's all right. We just want to know. Everyone wants to know.'

Tom said, when he saw the young man, 'I've lost Marigold – I don't want to lose Cora.'

'You won't lose Cora,' said the young man. 'It's just a fact-finding trip. I have a few clues.'

Cora rang up from Paris the next night, late. 'There's

been a probable sighting,' she said. 'That's all we can tell you.'

'Where?' said Tom.

'I mustn't say.'

'Well keep in touch – just a minute' – he turned to speak to Claire. 'They believe they've found a sighting.' Then, returning his voice to the phone, he said, 'If it's true, what a relief. Claire says, keep in touch with us. Do keep in touch.'

'Every day,' Cora promised.

'I hope,' said Claire to Tom, 'that those two are having a good time while they're about it.'

'So do I.'

When they were in England Tom and Claire lived in a large house at Wimbledon, in four acres of garden, well off the road. It had been built in 1932 and had always been occupied by film people – producers, film tycoons, stars of fame and substance.

For Jeanne, who had by no means given up her inscrutable campaign against Tom, the house itself was a provocation. In reality it frightened her, its size, its silence behind the curtained windows and closed doors, and its loftiness inside, in the circular entrance hall, on the few occasions that the door was opened to admit her.

'I want to see Mr. Richards.'

A new face had opened the door every time she had called. A series of young men, secretaries, helpers of the Richards family according as they were told off to open the door. Claire kept no live-in servants except the cook, also called Claire. But in the world of films there were always nice young girls, nice young men hanging around.

'Tom Richards is resting, I believe. You know he has to rest.'

'I'm Jeanne.'

'Oh yes, I recognised you. Would you like to see Mrs. Richards?'

'No, I saw her already.'

'Just take a seat, I'll see what I can do, Jeanne.'

Claire finally appeared as Jeanne knew she would.

'Come in and sit down. Have a drink.' They would go into a smaller room with drinks on the side table and a newspaper falling to bits on the floor.

'You know, Jeanne, we're worried about Marigold. Tom has had a lot of troubles. That last interview you gave wasn't very nice. Why did you do that? What have we done to you?'

'I've been used,' said Jeanne.

'We're all used,' Claire said.

'Oh, really? Well, explain why I'm the key figure in the film and I don't get star billing.'

'Because you are not the star,' said Claire. 'Rose Woodstock is the star.'

'I'm the main character in the story and I hardly have three close-ups. I *am* the story.'

'That's an artistic problem,' said Claire. 'You have had the opportunity of talking to Tom.'

'No, I haven't.'

'Well, you know Tom had an accident. Didn't you see the rushes ever?'

'No, I didn't. The directors didn't think I was worth asking.'

Claire pointed out that Jeanne had a contract. She should take it to her agent, her lawyer, if she thought she had a gripe. Claire pointed out everything except the fact that Jeanne was actually cast to have the fleeting part of 'Jeanne' in the film. A flash here and there and she was gone. It was difficult for Claire to be so explicit. It sounded deprecating. How does one explain an act of art? Rose Woodstock was the obvious dramatic draw, with her name, her looks and her outstanding presence. Never once had Jeanne been made to portray a rival to Rose. There was no story of female competition for the principal actor's affections. Jeanne was an idea. A hamburger girl, frequently with her back to the camera, whose part in the story was by definition that of a nobody.

'But I,' insisted Jeanne, 'am the one who's going to inherit, to be a millionairess.'

Claire thought the girl was mad. Her face was gaunt. Unlike the fairly pretty aspect she had presented in the film her look now was slightly haunted. Claire suspected she had been taking drugs. Jeanne had gone to Venice, to the Biennale film festival, aimlessly drawing to herself what attention she could, but unable to compete with Rose Woodstock or even to find a place at a café table with the glamorous, white-toothed leading male actor who, in the film, had so well known how to offer a present to a girl (Rose Woodstock), and who now, in Venice absolutely failed to recognise Jeanne.

Claire discerned that Jeanne urgently needed a psychiatrist's help.

'I was to have inherited millions.'

'Jeanne, you are not the Jeanne in the movie.'

'Oh, no?' said Jeanne. 'Oh, no?' This carried a threatening note. Claire thereupon decided not to give her any money, as she had been thinking of doing.

'You signed a contract,' Claire said rather harshly. 'Presumably you had an agent and you've been paid. Go and tell all this to your agent, Jeanne. We don't want you here.'

'And,' Jeanne went on, without moving, 'I was deliberately photographed in half-profile all the time, so I wouldn't be recognised. The light always, always, blotted me half out.'

'Light,' said Claire, 'is a director's problem if it's in the open air. You have to catch the same light from day to day to provide continuity. But anyway, you were meant to be half blotted out. That was the film. You could consult a lawyer if you aren't satisfied. But it's rather late. Why didn't you protest at the time?'

'Because I'm inexperienced. Because I didn't realise what was going on. I was exploited.'

Claire, not knowing if Tom had slept with the girl or not, maintained an air of kindly coolness and of other miraculous and contradictory qualities such as she had learnt to adopt in the course of her life with Tom: maternal extraneity, professional amateurism, understanding and incomprehension, yes and no.

Escorting Jeanne decisively to the door Claire said, 'Have you a family?'

'My mother was with me in Venice. We saw Marigold.'

'Really? Where?'

'In one of those lanes. She was with a man.'

'Can you describe him?'

'Fairly old. Like Tom. What sort of man can she expect? – Face like hers.'

'You should have reported this at the time,' said Claire. 'Interpol are looking for Marigold.'

'That's not my problem.'

'You're right.'

By instinct Claire had sworn off lovers until Marigold should be found. Like Tom, she felt that Marigold was still alive somewhere. Cora rang her up. After the first possible 'sighting' which was at Montmartre, she and bright young Ivan had received only vague 'signalisations', as Cora put it. In the meantime Ivan had set up an office in a small street near the rue de Rivoli. He held that if you set up an office in Paris for a project you were going about things the right way. An office, an informative-type computer, a fax machine, two telephones (one unlisted, one not). They were now in the way of receiving confidential information from any source. Marigold's face in many angles of photography had been planted with taxi-drivers, barmen, students and teachers, at numerous universities, especially those few where the students did not have to produce a school leaving certificate to sign up for a course. Cora and Ivan meanwhile stayed in a rented apartment on the Boulevard St. Germain. Cora wandered round the boutiques and department stores. Ivan, to do him justice, went to his office every day to check on the messages – many, but mostly futile – that arrived from his array of informers. Claire paid, and was well-satisfied with Ivan's efforts. She was sure he had given professional thought to the problem. She was sure he was very busy about it. But was Marigold still in Europe? She could be anywhere, anywhere . . .

'She is in Europe,' said Ivan decisively.

How did he know?

He wasn't saying. He just knew.

'I don't so much want to know where she is,' Claire told Cora. 'I only want to know if she's alive.'

'Or dead,' said Cora.

Claire hadn't liked to actually give voice to the alternative.

She suspected that Tom, too, had given up lovers. There seemed to be no women in his present life, but Claire didn't attach weight to that aspect of Tom's character. It was an extraordinary marriage, and Claire only reflected briefly on what Marigold had once visited her to say: 'Why don't you and Pa separate? Why don't you get divorced like other couples in your state?'

Well, thanks, Marigold. We are closer now than we ever were, Claire mused.

She had gone to the film festival at Venice with Tom.

The reporters asked Tom about Marigold: 'Your daughter. Her disappearance. What were your relations with Marigold? Not too good I gather.'

'That she's my daughter is one fact,' Tom replied to one of these enquiries. 'My relations with her are another. What I'm looking for is my daughter. You can keep your nose out of my relations.'

And Claire told them, 'We're doing everything in our

power to trace the whereabouts of Marigold. She is free to go where she likes. But her disappearance is worrying.'

Tom's film, *Unfinished Business*, was a decided success.

'But,' Tom told Dave, 'I didn't feel the usual warmth, the camaraderie. You would think the film people would come up to me and ask about Marigold, wouldn't you? Well, at least I must admit, Zeffirelli rang me up. "Tom," he said, "I read about Marigold. Don't give up. Keep your courage. She must be somewhere. If there's anything I can do . . ." You see,' said Tom, 'that's what I call a friend. Franco Zeffirelli is human and he feels for people. But the British, the Americans – they're so suspicious. Do they really think I've murdered Marigold, had her done away with? Is that what they do to their own daughters?'

'It's put in their minds by the newspapers. The diarists drop hints, as you can see.'

'But why?'

'It seems to me,' Dave said, 'that the tone is set by Marigold herself.'

'She's in touch with journalists, you mean?'

'That I don't know. But she could set the tone in a number of ways, Tom. Word of mouth is the strongest method I know, always has been.'

'Then you think my daughter's still alive.'

'Alive,' said Dave, 'and kicking.'

'Why should she want to foul-mouth me?' Tom said.

'She doesn't like you.' Dave stated this so much as a matter of fact that Tom wondered if he had some certain source of knowledge.

'Dave,' he said, 'if you suspect anything. If you could tell me where she is, or even give an indication . . .'

But Dave shook his head.

CHAPTER TWELVE

Let us go then, you and I, . . .

'You should write your memoirs.'

'I know,' Tom said. 'But you wouldn't believe how many chances of recording my memories I missed. So many conversations. All forgotten, and so many have died. John Braine knew a good deal about films, he had a whole lot to say, especially about films adapted from books. But I can't remember a single word of it, not one point that he raised. All I recall of John Braine is that he advised me to drink Earl Grey tea. Filthy stuff, to my taste. Then there was Mary McCarthy. She spoke voluminously but I don't remember a thing, didn't take a note. What I remember was how formal and conventional she was. At a cocktail party she always wore a correct dress, sometimes black, sometimes red, very smart, with a diamond brooch and white kid gloves. Always the white kid gloves which she held with her handbag. But who cares about details like those?'

'I care,' said Dave.

'Do you really! Do you honestly? – Why?'

'It tells you something about the person, details like Earl Grey tea and white kid gloves.'

'You're right,' Tom said. 'You're absolutely right. But I wouldn't have expected you to feel that way. In fact I think they wanted to create a memory of themselves – Earl Grey tea and white kid gloves.'

Two days after this, while Dave was alone in his taxi after dropping a fare at Holborn, a car drew up beside him at a traffic light. Dave glanced as he waited, at his neighbour, a young man with a nobody-special look and sun-glasses accompanied by a long-haired mousey girl, in a B.M.W. As he glanced back at the traffic light, now changing, he was aware of an arm coming out of the window of the B.M.W. and after that he was aware of little else – some hooting behind him urging his taxi to move – until he came to full consciousness in hospital. Dave had lost a small fragment of his skull, his chin was cut with glass from the broken window, he suffered from shock and concussion, but otherwise was sound. He was told his life had been saved by a fraction of an inch.

He could only vaguely describe the hit-man and the girl companion to the police. The car, he knew, was black and shiny, a three-year-old model.

Had he any enemies, debts? No, he hadn't. They searched his house from top to bottom, much to his wife's indignation: 'We're the victim and they treat us like the criminal.' The police found no drugs, no evidence of handling drugs, – they found nothing.

After Dave was discharged with his head still in bandages an inspector of police in plain clothes came to see him. The man took off his glasses, breathed on them one lens after the other, cleaned them with his handkerchief and put them on again.

'You are quite a friend of Tom Richards, aren't you?' said the policeman.

'That's a fact,' said Dave.

'I daresay you've wondered if this misfortune of yours might have some connection with him?'

'I've wondered,' Dave said. 'And so has he. We didn't want the press and the T.V. to get hold of the idea.'

'Well,' said the man, 'it's one of those cases where it even might be helpful if the press did catch on to it.'

'It could be anybody,' Dave said. 'How much can a hit-man cost?'

'A lot,' said the policeman.

'That leaves out a lot of people,' Dave said. 'If they wanted to get at Tom through me, the number is limited. If they only wanted to get at a taxi-driver, a Mr. Anybody on the street, like they do and you know it, there is no limit to the category of person.'

'Who are Tom Richards' enemies?'

'You have to ask him yourself. There are always cranks who want to hit the famous.'

'But they hit you.'

'Well, it could have meant a piece of advice for Tom and then again, it couldn't.'

'How are you feeling?'

'Pretty rotten. I've got a headache. I dream of the hospital, though. The lovely nurses.'

The press had been sympathetic, indignant, puzzled.

Tom said to Claire, 'We have too much money. It

allows us too many possibilities, endless options. It could be Marigold, quite easily. It's unlikely to be Jeanne although she would have some sort of motive. Jeanne couldn't afford it. Marigold could.'

'And Rose Woodstock?' Claire said.

'You can forget Rose. She got her prize at Venice, didn't she?'

'Yes, but you didn't wait to see her collect it.'

To the police, Tom said, 'It fills me with horror but I find the idea that the bullet which hit Dave was meant to intimidate me irresistible. What other reason should bring him into the news like this? What they're saying is "Next time it will be you, and we'll get you." But Why? Supposing Dave had been killed. Who would it serve? *Cui bono* as Cicero said.'

'We're a long way from Cicero's time. He probably didn't give much thought about the motiveless crime. I'm not up in Cicero,' said the inspector.

'The gratuitous gesture? Do you think it's that?' Tom said.

'Can't rule it out.'

They didn't say, but they plainly suspected, Marigold.

'Is there no way you can make your daughter come out in the open? She needs help. She's probably dangerous.'

'Perhaps if I separated from Claire. If we put in for a divorce, she might come out of hiding, if that's where she is. But even if we did that, she wouldn't be convinced. You know, we're neither of us at all sure but it could be Marigold who hired that killer in the B.M.W.'

'Have the police been back to see you?' Dave said on the phone to Tom.

'Yes.'

'What did they say?'

'Nothing. They talk in circles.'

'That's to trip you up,' said Dave. 'Second, third time round you're almost bound to contradict yourself.' He wanted very much to go cruising with Tom again.

'Let's wait awhile,' said Tom. He hated to be afraid.

Tom got out some photographs of Marigold. Marigold at sixteen in her tennis clothes. Marigold at a ball, frilled up in white. Marigold eating a frankfurter at a swimming-pool in New York State.

'She is not so hideous,' Tom said to Claire.

'She has a fairly good figure,' said Claire, looking at the photos that Tom had handed her. 'It's only the expression.'

'In fact,' said Tom, 'by modern standards she has quite an interesting face. Not a beauty. But interesting; photogenic. She would do well in a harsh movie. Say, Ibsen; say Ibsen, a film adaptation. Say Thomas Hardy. I wish I'd thought of it.'

'Has she ever had a film test?'

'Not that I know of,' said Tom. 'Not by me, anyhow. Those little eyes . . .'

'They make too much of the eyes in my opinion in modern films and T.V.,' Claire said. 'They can't get a decent script so they make it up with huge watery shining eyes brimming with feeling. Too much, too many –'

'Well, you could be right.'

Jeanne's lawyer wrote. Tom, he said, had represented to Jeanne that her role in *Unfinished Business* was to be a major one. He had actually put that in writing. 'Of major importance.' Instead, she had occupied a minor part. And so on. 'My client deserves an explanation with adequate compensation for the professional damages undergone.'

The lawyer was a well-known and expensive one, who would never have taken on such a doubtful case without a good down-payment. Where did Jeanne get the money?

'Probably Marigold,' said Claire. 'It was a mistake on my part to ever settle money on her. But as she's my daughter . . .'

In the course of their enquiries with the shooting of Dave, an ex-boyfriend of Marigold's emerged. Now discarded, he was the same man as was concealed with her in the trailer when Tom and Claire went to look for her in the Haute Savoie. That was now four months ago. The youth recounted his experience with Marigold but said they had parted shortly afterwards. He did not discount that Marigold was perfectly capable of hiring a hit-man if the plan suited her. The police eventually believed the boy, whose name for the present purpose is irrelevant, and let him go. Where was Marigold? Nobody knew for sure.

Cora and Ivan had by now set up an efficient office in Paris fitted with more sophisticated investigative equipment and information-receivers, where clues, indications and probable sightings of Marigold were abundantly recorded. Ivan no longer claimed she was still in Europe. She had been seen in Peru, in Cochin and parts of Southern India, she had been seen in Georgetown, Washington and in Pakistan.

Cora's brief affair with Marigold's brother-in-law Ralph was over. Claire had somehow got him a managerial job, a better one than he had before. He had returned to his wife, Ruth, who had no inkling of his affair with Cora and refused to believe it when Jeanne rang her up to tell her.

'Back to reality,' he said at the first sign of a return of his impotence with Ruth. She was annoyed.

Cora was fascinated by her new boyfriend, Ivan the investigator, and their flat in Paris. Marigold had become part of their career.

Tom sought a meeting with the boyfriend of the camping-site, he who had last been known to see and speak to Marigold in the flesh. 'Put word round,' Tom said, 'that when she turns up I intend to star her in a film. I think her star quality. She is photogenic. I never realised it, but she is. Put round the word. I will show footage of her face. Not on paternal grounds. On artistic grounds.'

'Put round where?' said the young man. 'I haven't a clue who she sees.'

'Have a try,' said Tom, handing him an envelope. The money was received without comment, stuffed into a pocket of a young man's jeans, perhaps to bear fruit, perhaps not.

'If she turns up,' said Tom, 'I will do everything she wants, short of supporting drugs or terrorist activities.'

'Why do you say that?'

'I owe no explanation.'

Cora faxed that Marigold had been seen for certain in Brazil in a clinic for plastic surgery. 'Be quick,' Cora wrote, 'as she's definitely there now, having a face change.'

As with the other sightings this proved to be a false alarm. 'Marigold,' Tom observed to Claire, 'would in any case never change her face. When she looks in the glass she does not see the interesting face that she has, she sees absolute beauty, I'm convinced. Love is blind.'

It was possible, he knew, that some of the sightings – there was a very likely one in Cork – were genuine. But the investigators always got there a day too late. She had been, yes. But she had gone.

Tom's lawyer, Fortescue-Brown on the phone: 'Can you look in at the office or can you make it convenient for me to come to you?'

'What about?' said Tom.

'That change in your will. It's been in abeyance for some months.'

'What change in my will?'

'What you called me about when you were in hospital. There was a girl involved. I hope, in fact, you've thought it over.'

'Girl?' – He must mean the hamburger girl. Tom marvelled at his past dream, now exhausted by the reality of the film and his actual boredom with the tiresome, real Jeanne. 'Forget the alterations to the will,' he said.

'Scrap them all?'

'All. They're a thing of the past.'

In fact, Tom was immersing himself into an altogether new story for a film.

Let us go then, you and I, . . .

He was indulging one of his favourite dream-games: 'If Julius Caesar came back to life, you take him up in a lift, you take him up in an aeroplane. What would his reaction be? Caesar would have understood Ascot but an electric kettle would have had him foxed. You bring back the Brontës and stage a rock-concert outside their house at Haworth. What would their reaction be? You bring back Sophocles and play him Mahler's Symphony No. 1 . . .'

'There's no end to it,' said Dave. 'No end to it.'

Historical shifts had started fertilising in Tom's mind. 'My new film,' he eventually told Dave, 'is set in Roman Britain towards the end of the occupation, around the fifth century A.D. I have this centurion, he really doesn't want to uproot himself, Britain has been his family's home for over two centuries. His brothers and cousins are mainly civil servants and might stay on. But my man is in the army, he has to go. Orders from Rome. The legions were needed to defend Rome at that period, you see.'

'I better look it up in the encyclopaedia. What's his name?' said Dave.

'I don't know yet. Call him Paul. Call him anything. He's married with children. He has a servant, a Celt, a native of Britain. That's what the story is going to be about, mainly.'

'Is he gay?'

'No. But he's devoted to his Celt who is a most eccentric type. The wife tolerates the friendship, but his daughter, no. She's a fierce one. Striking looks, not good-looking in fact plain ugly. But striking. Jealous, fierce, vindictive through and through.'

'Sounds like Marigold,' said Dave.

'Now that you mention it, yes,' Tom said. 'In fact I would offer Marigold the part if I ever set eyes on her again.'

'Would she accept?'

Tom paused to think this over quite a long time. Eventually, he said, 'I don't know. I really don't know. Perhaps not.' Tom reached out and took the photograph of Marigold that he had given to Dave to prop up in the front of the taxi, just in case Dave should come across her in his day's work.

'Has it occurred to you,' Dave said, 'that Marigold has a psychological problem? Really and truly, Tom, she can't be altogether right.'

'I never actually thought much of that,' Tom said, studying the photograph.

'They say you don't, with your nearest kin. It's the last thing you think of. The realisation sometimes comes slowly.'

'I'll talk to Claire. It could be. You know, I wonder if she's alive and if so, where she is.' Tom slipped back the photograph. Marigold did look not quite balanced; something about the eyes.

'Too rich,' said Dave. 'You see on the T.V. shows, people looking for missing persons. They're nearly all poor. They find missing people at the railway station, at cafés, in bars, at bus-stops. That's the sort of place where they are sighted. But Marigold ... Has she touched her money?'

'Not that we know of. But we don't know of all the places, the countries, where she could have kept her money.'

Tom's centurion and Celt continued to amplify in his thoughts and mind. The story was already like a tree; it put out branches, sprouted leaves.

Cedric (provisional name of the Celt – Tom made a note 'Look up names, see if Cedric is right for the period.') was to be gifted with second sight. He could see into the future, the near future to give plausibility to his forecasting capacities, and the distant future, which sounded quite crazy, dangerously so in those days of popular suspicions and superstitions. Tom's Celt could 'see' for instance, the Field of the Cloth of Gold, the building of Versailles, the discovery of Florida. Wildest of all, he could see men walking on the moon. This last vision he was to be warned about. Diana, the goddess of the moon, was still a considerable political force in the Roman Empire and beyond. And here in Britain the Druids ruled the people. Tom's Celt babbled about motor-bikes. He could also foresee tomorrow's weather with an accuracy which would incense the Druids. As the centurion and his Celt took shape as characters Tom grew more and more enthusiastic, convinced he had a first-class film idea. He would have to map out the story, prepare a treatment, raise money, think of casting. It made Tom very happy to be once more lost in his profession.

'I need a strong hard woman. Fierce.' (His Celt's lover.) 'Someone like Marigold,' he told Dave.

'I'll have to shoot in Northumberland and in Italy,' Tom told Claire. 'The Italian part should be pleasant for you.'

'I'll come,' said Claire.

Sometimes Tom had the feeling that Marigold was quite nearby. According to Cora and Ivan, still lingering in Paris, sightings were still being reported on their network. She had been 'seen' in Greece, Puerto Rico and Vienna all in one week. Since the shooting of Dave Interpol had taken an interest in finding her; how deep their enquiries went no one would know.

'They should pack up that Paris office,' Tom said to Claire. 'It's a useless extravagance.'

'Let them enjoy themselves a little longer.' He knew she meant by this to put in a plea for Tom not to be a spoil-sport.

CHAPTER THIRTEEN

In the uncertainty of Marigold's being dead or alive, her husband, James, told everyone he felt he should not press the subject of divorce. He came to see Claire one late afternoon. She poured him a drink. She looked at him and wondered, 'Could he possibly have murdered her?' His whereabouts at the time of her disappearance had been vaguely on the American continent. It was a question that inevitably passed through her mind whenever she saw, or even thought of, anyone who had been connected with Marigold. James was aged thirty-nine, clever, balding, with big dark-framed glasses and the trace of a beard. He appealed to Claire less, now, than he ever did. However, she thought it unlikely that he should have killed a wife, presumably for gain, when he could get money out of her any other way.

Tom had faith in James's scholarship. He had recently appointed him technical adviser on early Roman sites, for his new film.

Claire said, 'Have you seen the police lately, James?'

He did not immediately reply. Then, 'Oh, you mean about Marigold? No, they've left me alone.'

For some reason Claire didn't like the sound of 'No, they've left me alone.' Nor was she easy with his answer to her next question. 'Are you prepared to have another try with Marigold?'

He looked puzzled. 'Another try with Marigold?'

'When she comes back.'

'Oh, when she comes back. Look, Claire, I don't think she'll ever come back to me.'

'Do you mean you don't think she'll ever come back at all?'

'No, I don't mean that. My guess is as good as yours as to what's happened to her, and I've no way of guessing, no clue.'

Claire saw she had probed enough. It was unfair that everyone concerned with Marigold was obliged to suspect everyone else. 'If she's doing this deliberately,' Claire said, 'I'll never talk to her again. If she has fallen foul of someone and is dead, I'll never forgive myself.'

'Why wouldn't you forgive yourself?'

'I don't know, I really don't know,' said Claire. 'It can happen that you have a sense of guilt about somebody without having done anything in that regard.'

She was relieved to hear him say, 'I know what you mean. I feel exactly the same way about Marigold. Perhaps she wants us to feel guilt.'

'Perhaps. In fact, Tom refuses to feel guilty. We can do no more than we are doing to find Marigold. Tom says he refuses to distort his soul by suppressing his true experience of his daughter just for appearances.'

'I'm glad of that,' James said. 'I'm glad he's given me this wonderful job. It might have been construed as disloyalty to Marigold. Everyone knows our marriage was splitting up.'

'Tom is very professional,' Claire said. 'He wants the best people, always, for his film. And you're the best available historical researcher for the present film. Besides, he's convinced that Marigold hired the hit-man.'

'Yes, I think she would do that.'

'You think she would?'

'Yes, she would,' said James. 'I was married to her a very short time but I did learn not to count on her equilibrium.'

What they were both wondering was, 'What could she do next?'

The title of the film was to be *Watling Street*, the name of the old Roman road stretching diagonally across the south-west of England; although this was not a Roman name, Tom's Celt was able to foresee that the charming name of the famous road was Watling Street from the ninth century onwards under the occupation by Danish forces.

The street itself stretched from the present Hyde Park Corner in London to Wroxeter near Shrewsbury. Wroxeter was at the time of Tom's centurion the city of Viroconium, remains of which still exist. Now, the Celt 'saw' in advance whenever he tuned in, everything that happened in Watling Street as he himself called the road. He babbled about a 'self-service laundry at Maida Vale', about a 'battle of Bosworth Field between Tamworth and Hinckley'; he raved about the goings-on at 'The Black Swan' at Grendon. He said it was cold at Lichfield three miles off Watling Street under black and grey puff clouds. It was, he said, a heavy, undulating landscape. There was a wild animal collection at Whipsnade. Tom made long notes about what his Celt foresaw 'in the year 433 A.D. on the site of the future Watling Street.' He was intent on writing at least the first draft of the script. Under 'Possible Names Early Britons' he listed 'Morgan, Bronwyn, Iolo, Huffa, Cedric, Gareth.' For the centurion he stuck to his first thought 'Paulus Aurelius', for the Celt, Cedric was changed to Dennis, then back to Cedric again.

Cedric the Celt had to be a star, but one with a strong wild face, the face of a young man sent mad by complete knowledge of the future, and yet with little control over his own life, belonging as he did to his centurion. And the centurion, Paulus Aurelius? Tom did his best not to model him on himself, or at least on his own self-image, but finding this was impossible he gave in and decided he could compose better if he was the model for Paulus Aurelius – what the hell? Then Tom couldn't sleep at nights. For a week he puzzled over the casting of Cedric the Celt. Night after night before his closed eyes, and practically on his pillow in the morning, looking at him, looking ... he could see the dark sullen ugly face of Marigold, herself. 'I know of no star to resemble her,' he said to Claire, 'but she haunts my dreams as the Celt, Cedric the sorcerer. I feel he would look just like her. It's absurd there are no star actresses like her.'

'Get someone, anyone, any boy,' said Claire, 'and make an actor of him.'

'Easier said than done,' said Tom.

Let us go then, you and I, . . .

He explained to Dave what he was looking for. 'A squat dark fellow. If possible hardly any neck. Deep-set tiny black eyes. He could have a kindliness about him but he has the tragic future written on his face. He belongs to the world of legend and yet he is alive and real in the fifth century.'

'I'll keep a look out,' said Dave.

'It's unlikely you'll find anyone like it,' said Tom. 'But remember Marigold's photo. Keep it in front of you.'

'It might not be so unlikely,' Dave said. 'You know there are a few youths around who look like what you want. A few more than you might think.'

'They would have to act,' said Tom.

'That would be up to you,' said Dave in his wisdom.

Charlie Good, Claire's late and most recent lover, was having a snack lunch in a pub in Gloucestershire when he saw Marigold doing the same. Charlie was a free-lance physiotherapist. He had lived-in with Claire in their capacious house at Wimbledon all the time Tom had been disabled. Tom had first suspected his presence in the house by the promptness with which Charlie appeared on the occasions when his own physiotherapist and masseur was absent a day, or held up for some reason. 'I'll get Charlie,' Claire would say, and without much delay Charlie would appear with his jars of aromatics by Tom's bedside or beside his chair. Claire had hardly bothered to cover Charlie's presence as a permanent guest. She had parted amicably from Charlie, and in a way that suited him, by the time Tom began to get about again.

When he came across Marigold, however, Charlie Good was getting short of funds, a condition which was more or less a chronic norm with him. Perhaps shortage of money sharpened his eyes: he noticed, first, a sullen-looking youth at a corner table. A bad face, he thought, I wouldn't trust *him*. The youth wore a brown leather jacket over a grey jersey and a check shirt, blue jeans, heavy, black, muddy boots. But something about the hands, the hands . . . Charlie looked more carefully and discerned Marigold. He looked away, pretending to be lost in his dreams; he looked into his beer. He ordered another and remarked to the landlord on the filthy weather.

Charlie drank his beer and left the pub. He went out to his ancient Rover and there he waited among the other vehicles, five of them, drawn up outside the pub. The rain was heavy. Marigold appeared. Charlie ducked. She made for a camper, gave a melancholy look around, got in and drove off. Charlie followed her and watched her dive into a sad field next to a cemetery.

CHAPTER FOURTEEN

The reports from the Paris 'organisation' or 'network' as Cora and Ivan called it – sightings of Marigold in Honolulu, or up the Amazon as they might be – were regularly passed on to the police by Tom. It could have been that these dazzling place-names had waylaid the bored investigators from visualising Marigold in some funk-hole nearer home. Big-moneyed daughters don't live in sordid, damp discomfort, and if disguised as boys they would likely be living with another transvestite or such like, not alone.

Claire had all along opposed Tom's desire to trace Marigold through the police, and now that she was wanted for questioning about the hit and run attack on Dave, Claire was even less keen on the idea. She would not own that Marigold could be responsible for an act of criminal violence. She told Tom, 'You would incriminate your own daughter before you knew the facts.'

'But she's mad, don't you see that?' Tom was thinking

of Dave in the hospital, his brown worn face on the pillow, with his head in bandages, trying not to show pain or fear. 'It was nearly murder, very near,' said Tom.

Charlie Good, having located Marigold, went neither to her parents nor the police. He went to a television network and for a fair fee conducted them to the field where Marigold was camped.

Tom, at that hour, was in Dave's sitting room in Camberwell having a cup of tea, as he sometimes did before or after a meditative cruising session. Dave's wife, slim, fair-skinned, always amiable to Tom whom she liked tremendously, turned on the television news. Tom always liked to watch news.

A crowd of excited journalists, a number of onlookers ... The name 'Marigold' ... A police car ... A close-up of a young man, yes, but it could be a girl, and anyway it was Marigold. She was making a statement. 'I'm free to do what I like, live where I want. I don't know anything about any shooting. I've been living like this in order to experience at first hand what it's like to be destitute. After my work in the field of redundancy I decided to write a book. Few realise what redundancy can lead to. Loss of home, loss of social background. Complete destitution. Some people I know live in their cars. With their dogs for protection and company. The people round here have been very good to me. They bring me food and even calor gas.' The camera beamed on a young woman holding a white plastic supermarket bag with the top of a loaf of bread sticking out. 'I had no idea that Jimmy was Marigold. We always knew her as Jimmy. But she's doing no-one no harm, and living in dignity. I just brought her a few provisions.' Gently enough, Marigold was then led away to a police car.

'Where is all this going on? Did you hear?' said Tom.

'I didn't catch it,' said Dave. 'But anyway, you know she's alive and she's explaining herself all right.'

Tom got up slowly from the sofa, for his back still gave him trouble when he sat on a low seat. 'I better phone Claire,' he said.

Within a few days Marigold had become a national folk heroine. The papers announced:

Marigold Found!

Millionaire Film Magnate's daughter lives rough to show solidarity with the out-of-works.

The police could find nothing whatsoever to connect her with the shooting of Dave. She gave interviews such as Tom and Claire could only admire: Why was she passing herself off as a man? – Partly for self-protection, she said. Partly, she wanted to be unrecognised and left alone. 'Besides, it's the men who mostly suffer from redundancy. I wanted to actually *feel* the situation. Somehow the gulf between rich and poor, between employed and jobless must be bridged. Increased unemployment is leading the country to disaster.'

'She means it,' said Claire. 'I'm sure she means every word. I've had a long conversation with her.'

Cora returned to London declaring she had never worked so hard in her life. 'Ivan is keeping on the office. There are so many missing persons, and now that he has the set-up it would be foolish to waste it.'

'He didn't get very far with Marigold,' said Tom.

'Oh, he would have got there in the end, I'm sure of that,' said Cora. But she was glad to be back in her flat in London. She told Claire that she was tired of living with all Ivan's electronic equipment, which had spilled over into their flat. Which meant she was tired of Ivan. He was soon to be part of the unwanted equipment, something of the past.

Marigold was back in her house.

'I still feel guilty about Dave,' Tom said. 'That shooting had something to do with me, I'm sure.' Claire, as he spoke, was busy. He felt a wave of deep affection for her. What would he do, he wondered, without Claire with her old-fashioned charity ledgers and her card indexes, wearing her Chanel suits and her Worth scent (*Je Reviens*)? For Claire he even tolerated that other Claire in the kitchen with her unspeakable food, her beetroots and her Beef Stroganoff and her spotted dumpling bilge.

Marigold had taken possession of the large cottage in Surrey where she had shared her brief married life with James. When he was not away on his literary travels he was in the habit of using the cottage as his headquarters, and now that Marigold had reappeared it seemed fair that the cottage should become part of the arrangement for their inevitable divorce. The house had been a wedding present to them both from Claire.

Marigold, now busy with a ghost-writer on her recent experiences as an out-of-work down-and-out, had no objection to recompensing James for his share of the house and any other important joint possessions arising from their marriage. A violent row had broken out between them, however, on the proprietorship of *Coleridge's Poetical Works*, Vols. I and II which Marigold claimed had been meant as a present for her alone by a school friend, and which James insisted was part of their joint wedding-present haul. The resulting argument, incongruous though it actually was in view of the book's minor value, reached the ears of the ghost-writer two rooms away. All the venom these two people had stored against each other was spurted out in the cause of this quite replaceable book, which neither party cherished for any particular reason. The book of poems was in any case presently lost sight of under the mounting heap of recriminations from both sides.

'Bitch and hermaphrodite!'

'Exploiter of women!'

'Instigator of murder!'

'Failed writer! Now you have to come begging a job from my father.'

'He's lucky to get me. What about you? – You should talk. Getting an important part just to keep you quiet. What chance would you ever have had to star in a film if you hadn't been Tom Richards' daughter?'

'Part? – I have no part in any film.'

Nevertheless, that was how Marigold came to learn that Tom had thought of giving her a part.

'Pa, is it true you have a part for me?' she said on the phone, later.

'Yes it is. A male part.' He no longer wanted Marigold to play a 'strong hard woman'. He wanted her for Cedric the Celt himself. 'You did it so well on the campsite I don't see why you shouldn't do well for me. I thought of it even before you turned up.'

'A male part. You think I'm a hermaphrodite?'

'Don't be silly. I've known you since you were born. But remember Shakespeare put men into female roles. I don't see why a girl can't play a boy, a very special boy, an ancient Briton. Elizabeth Bergner played the boy David in a play of the thirties. She was terrific.'

Marigold polished off her book through the ghost-writing agency she was dealing with. She had moved back to her mews flat in London, bringing with her nothing but *Coleridge's Poetical Works*, Vols. I and II, and leaving James to have what pickings he wanted from the cottage in Surrey. He was furiously angry, but there was nothing he could do but pack his suits, bring round the removal vans and see his lawyers.

He told Tom, 'Marigold is exasperating.'

'I know,' Tom said. 'She has too much money, that's the trouble with her. But she's going to make a marvellous prophet-Celt. Fortunately she knows how to work, she likes work.'

It was typical of Tom, and in a way a part of the mores of that world of dreams and reality which he was at home in, the world of filming scenes, casting people in parts, piecing together types and shadows, facts and illusions, that he made no distinction between divorced members of his family and those still married. That James and Marigold were breaking up meant nothing compared to James's value as location researcher. Marigold's dramatic disappearance and the discomfort it had caused were completely lost in the enthusiasm Tom felt for his hermaphroditic Celt of the years *c*. 436.

Rose Woodstock wanted to star. She had won an important award in Tom's last film. She was good box-office. Tom and his producers snapped her up to play the part of the centurion's wife, the Celt's lover perhaps. Rose was once more ravishing in Tom's eyes.

And Jeanne, his late hamburger girl, who no longer haunted him except through her lawyer's office – Claire had a good idea for keeping her quiet. 'Give her a flash-forward part, just a glimpse. That's all she's good for, but she's quite effective at that. Why don't you make the Celt foresee the French Revolution? Jeanne could play Marie-Antoinette. That would flatter her. Marie-Antoinette on the way to her execution, and a flash forward at the scaffold? How good Jeanne would be!'

Jeanne signed up for this part amicably, just as though she had never threatened Tom with legal action through the tough lawyer. That was the world they lived in.

Marigold was photographed and publicised in the early, preparatory, stages of the film. She had entered the national consciousness. It was often said privately that her disappearance had been a publicity stunt to work up interest in *Watling Street*. And when this was suggested publicly on a talk-show, she denied it vehemently. Her experiences were real sufferings, she explained, and her book would explain the rest. Which it did, and went into several fat editions. *Out of Work in a Camper* gave Marigold a glamour which Tom could only admire.

'I think she's more ambitious than I am,' Tom said to Dave.

'Can you trust her?' Dave said.

'That I don't know.'

They had reached a point in the film where the question was, normally, irrelevant. Actors were not at this stage trustworthy or otherwise. They functioned or they didn't. But Marigold?

Tom watched Marigold launching her book on a late night talk-show. She was so different, in this professional job, from what she had been in that awful home-movie of hers. He admired her magnetism, so that it didn't matter that as a woman she looked hideous – quite deliberately so. She described with bitter passion her adventures looking for a job, insults levelled at her and the people she 'represented', insolent interrogations. Whether these were real or invented, they made good televised material. She was quite expert, even when mouthing her most banal pronouncements: 'Psychiatrists tell us that redundancy based on poor performance often leads to feelings of guilt and even to suicide.' There was something about the way in which she said 'suicide', with a half-grin showing her top gums, that made Tom wonder if Marigold would stay with the film. She was capable of disappearing again. He decided to take all the necessary shots of Marigold: this was not an uncommon method of filming. In fact, very few directors shot in the sequences of the story. It often happened when an actor was pre-engaged for another film or an actress was pregnant, or if a special type of outdoor lighting had to be caught within a short season, or for economic reasons, that the director did not film in accordance with the A to Z principle. The scenes involving Marigold, Tom decided, must be done right away if one wanted to be on the safe side. The

Celt was to be assassinated by superstitious zealots in the end. Tom thought Marigold would look well, dead. He watched her face in the oblong frame of his television set. In any case, he always liked to visualise his actors in frames, as they would be eventually. Perhaps he could get Marigold to put on that part-smile as she pronounced the word 'suicide'. It would suit her 'dead' look. So Tom mused while Marigold on the late talk went on about 'the E.T.' (Employment Training, as you were supposed to have gathered) and 'the J.W.S.A.' (Job plan Workshop Standard Agreement). Tom started next morning, early, filming Marigold as the Celt in every phase of the film.

'Are you afraid I might walk out, Pa?' she said.

'Yes, I am.'

In ten days it was done. Marigold as Cedric the Celt lay finally with her eyes upturned, three daggers in her blood-stained tunic, and her lips forming a half-smile over the word 'suicide' silently formed. It was a relief to Tom to get her safely captured in at least the minimum footage, although he asked her (ordered her in fact as was his way) to 'stick around the set as there will be considerable re-takes.'

Rose Woodstock was never very happy while making a film unless she was sleeping with the director. It was a way of directing the film herself, or at least she felt it to be so.

Two weeks into the rehearsals of *Watling Street* Tom Richards was once more enamoured of Rose. She was now very blonde for her part as the British wife of the

Roman centurion. Her new colouring gave her a new type of glamour. He did not discourage the idea that she had a supreme and special say in his movie.

When Rose had first deserted Kevin Woodstock for him, Tom had felt some compunction. It was true that Rose had been married to Kevin for eleven years, a stretch of time when a separation could be expected, especially in the world of the cinema. But Tom respected Kevin for what he was, a professional, though mediocre, television director, specialising mainly in unusual synchronisations of sound. But Rose had moved from Kevin to Johnny Carr, obviously a temporary arrangement, so that Tom had now no qualms at all about monopolising Rose.

Tom thought of Johnny Carr as a good-looking loser. He was not greatly surprised when his lovely Cora, on abandoning her Paris adventure, shacked up again with Johnny, even while their divorce papers were being processed. She moved in with Johnny naturally and casually, presumably while waiting to decide on her next man.

Tom continued to marvel at Cora's beauty. He remembered sometimes how he had escorted both daughters up the aisle at their weddings. To what end? He and Claire had been married in a registry office and were still together, had never been provoked one by the other into a separation.

'Have you thought of leaving Claire?' Rose asked him.

'Yes, I have thought. But the answer is No.'

Kevin Woodstock had been questioned closely by the police at the time of Marigold's disappearance. He was then considered to be the last person to have seen Marigold. He was questioned again when Dave was shot by the unknown hit-man. It was Dave himself who insisted on the possibility of Kevin's guilt.

'Why Kevin Woodstock?'

'Because Tom Richards has gone off with his wife.'

But Rose herself told the police, 'That's ridiculous. I left Kevin of my own accord. We have parted amicably.'

Tom told Dave, 'Even if Marigold should walk out now she can't sabotage the film. I have all the necessary sequences featuring her. I'll want more, but in the meantime I've taken this precaution. Rather as one does with very old actors.'

'You did right,' said Dave.

'I hope you don't think I'm down on the girl.'

'Well, you are a bit. But you can't be blamed. She's unreliable.'

'I want her as Cedric to foresee a few more things. Events of everyday life. A journalist in the twentieth century in Budapest being condemned to twenty years in prison. I thought of my Celt having a vision of Marcel and Odette walking in the Bois de Boulogne but these are people out of a novel. They are fiction, not fact, a pity, because it would have made a charming scene.'

'Stick to fact,' said Dave. 'Don't get carried away!'

'Good advice,' said Tom. 'I want that Celt to foresee Charlie Chaplin.'

Tom was now having difficulties with Jeanne who was not at all pleased with Tom's interpretation of her role as Marie-Antoinette, seen through Cedric's eyes, on the way to the scaffold. The flash-forward showed Jeanne in the tumbril made up to look like the drawing of the desperate Queen by the painter David – without her wig, her hair ragged and *gamin*-style, her face prematurely old. Not at all unlike the original hamburger girl. Whereas Jeanne had wanted an opulent form of death-procession, with high-dressed hair, silks and ruffles. An important, glamorous execution. Jeanne had played the part as Tom wanted it; in fact, being thoroughly sulky, she played it well. But having seen the rushes she was fairly furious.

It was not long after Tom had resumed his love affair with Rose that Dave said:

'I can't take you around any more, Tom. Rose Woodstock is dangerous. Kevin Woodstock is still her husband. I don't trust him and I don't want another bullet through my head. My wife wants me to quit this taking you around. Perhaps she's right.'

'But Rose hasn't been living with Kevin for nearly a year. Perhaps more than a year, I don't know. She's recently been with my daughter's ex-husband Johnny Carr. Rose is getting divorced from Kevin, I'm sure. She deserves better than either of them. Carr is a born drop-out and Kevin Woodstock is a mediocrity.'

'Reason how you like,' said Dave, 'but someone shot me it seems as a warning to you, and they haven't got the man. Kevin Woodstock seems to me to fit the part. I'm going on my way, Tom.'

When he came to think of it seriously it also seemed to Tom, that Kevin fitted the part. He was out of work and in need of money. Supposing Marigold had commissioned him to take this wild action? For Kevin the motives would be jealousy, resentment, and the need for money. For Marigold . . . one didn't think of motives; she was a murky proposition. To think of her at all was a great inconvenience to Tom, especially now that he had registered her part in *Watling Street*, and was busy putting the film together with Rose, the Irish actor who was playing the part of the centurion, and a large supporting cast. It was an inconvenience to have to cope with Jeanne and her complaints: he had reluctantly enlarged her part to include some shots of Marie-Antoinette at the height of her glamour, in which Jeanne was all right but no more than all right. Tom's affair with Rose Woodstock was his present source of pleasure and sweetness. He had an extra-long new part written in for her, which included more close-ups than Tom normally cared for.

At intervals, especially now that Tom no longer went cruising with Dave, he turned up at his house in Wimbledon. He sometimes found Claire at home, and would spend an evening with her.

'Marigold is writing another book. It's to be called *Shock and Despair: A Study of Redundancy To-day*,' Tom said.

'I hope she gets a better ghost-writer this time.'

'She comes into the studio almost every day. Do you think she's happy?'

'Oh, God, no,' said Claire. 'She'd be miserable if she was happy. She's been working up Jeanne against you.'

'I sort of imagined that,' Tom said. 'I've had to extend Jeanne's part as Marie-Antoinette but I might cut it out in the end. I don't want the Celt, Cedric, to foresee only important historic moments, but fragments of the future, apparently disconnected. For instance, he has a clairvoyant moment in the sight of Michelangelo putting the finishing touches on his sculpture *Moses*. According to legend Michelangelo said to his statue "Speak to me." That's the sort of vignette I'm putting in. I don't need Jeanne and her vulgar Marie-Antoinette frills to tell me how to make a movie.'

'Tom, you know how it is. Agree with everyone, but have your own way finally.'

'Oh, yes. But it's wearing. I hate to have enemies.'

'I don't think you have enemies,' Claire said.

'No? Then who took that shot at Dave, and why?'

CHAPTER FIFTEEN

'For a spectacular like this I need a crane,' Tom said.

'There are those wonderful new cameras,' said one of the cameramen. 'Cranes are really out, Tom.'

'Nonsense, I need a crane. I have to direct the Battle of Agincourt. I have to take shots of those helicopters that Cedric sees in his dreams. I have to know from above, from some mountain, what's going on down there in the fort on Hadrian's Wall where they are sorting and sifting the grain.'

'Well, Tom, I should think you had enough of the crane last time.'

'This time I'll fasten the safety belt. I've borrowed a mobile crane, like the one they sold, a Chapman. I hope the technicians are up to moving it about. If not, hire the experts.'

*　　*　　*

Tom was on location in Northumberland filming a sequence of a Roman British fort at Hadrian's Wall, a busy scene in the courtyard of a specially-constructed inn and, after that, a rowdy scene at a fair. Rose Woodstock as the centurion's British wife, so tall, so fair and beautiful, crossed the courtyard between a milkmaid with a pole across her shoulders bearing up a pail on each side, and a boy piling wood in neat, efficient rows. She was next seen at the fair, moving from stall to stall in the fruit market and at the pastry-cook's. Marigold, as Cedric, in her rough knee-length tunic, cross-strapped legging sandals and her sullen glitter-eyed look, stood against a tree contemplating the centurion's lovely wife. The latter turns her head and catches the gaze of the dark sooth-sayer. (A repeat shot, for Marigold had already posed under a tree looking at nothing – 'in case'.) 'O.K. *Cut.*'

Work stopped early. They started early with the light just right for continuity. By six in the morning the long shed which was headquarters was already alive with actors and their preparatory activities. Tom arrived promptly. At this stage in the film he was no longer an object of awe. No hush greeted him as he came into the shed, which satisfied him greatly. It meant that work was proceeding seriously. There was hardly a square foot of the shed unoccupied. It seemed that everyone was changing their clothes, or, being young children, being changed by their mothers or minders. In a corner at a table, sat the music man, touching up a piece of music. Along one side of this location-studio a row of dressing tables had been fixed, each with a mirror encircled by fierce lights. The make-up men and women were busy on the actors, dabbing light and shade on their faces, splashing them with artful, cosmetic mud, tracing deep wound marks, pock-marks, brushing out their hair, making them into Roman soldiers or early Britons.

'They look too clean,' Tom would often say, 'too well-fed. In Roman Britain the children would often be dirty and skinny, with bad teeth. Can't you at least make their teeth look bad?' He knew they could do this, and that they would scatter a touch of 'decay' among the healthy teeth of the minor and meaner actors.

Enough for now of the British fort. On with a French crowd scene. 'My Colossal' Tom said, referring to the film. In fact he hated crowd scenes, but had decided to do as many as he could in Northumberland where he had hired a lot of space. The cast was indeed colossal, but he loved his very long, very high barn and the caravans that he and the principal actors worked from. Cedric the Celt is made to see and describe a 'helicopter' from which (Tom's crane) can be filmed a shot of a border skirmish, – a small crowd of marauding Danes. Tom's crane, which had been lugged carefully to Northumberland, was one of his real joys on that location.

He had to have a meeting with his producers, the men with the money, in London; he went there at the week-end accompanied by Rose Woodstock. As a large box-office participant, Rose, with her lawyer, attended the meeting, which took place on Saturday afternoon. Tom had been looking forward to spending the evening alone with Rose, dining at some glamorous night-spot where Rose loved to be seen, then afterwards to her flat for the night. She was, in fact, well-disposed to this idea. But something about financial meetings and the sight and sound of top stars discussing their percentages of gains (which they called their percentuals), always put Tom off the romantic side of his life. Rose was not at all pleased when he told her he would have to spend the evening 'discussing something' with Claire. 'I wanted to discuss a new part to be written-in for me.'

Tom knew she would immediately get hold of someone else to go out with, perhaps someone younger and more exciting. But he was Tom Richards; he could not help his moods.

Claire was not in the house. She was out for dinner. Tom made himself comfortable with a sandwich and a glass of wine. What a fool I am! he thought, as he realised he had probably done permanent damage to his love-affair with gorgeous Rose. But at the same time he knew there had been nothing he could do to change events. He had been overtaken by a moral distaste for Rose Woodstock, and even that was probably unjust. She was perfectly entitled to make an attempt to alter a contract in her own favour; she was justified in having a lawyer by her side when she did business. But it had put Tom off; he could not change his nature.

Nor could he be more than icily pleasant to Claire the cook when she offered him her attentions. 'I have some boeuf bourguignon all ready,' she said, practically licking her lips about it. 'My nephew's here on a visit.'

'I want a sandwich and a glass of red wine. A ham sandwich. Definitely, that's all.'

His wife, Claire, he reflected in his dark thoughts, had been brought up between Claridges and the Paris

Ritz. Claire was a woman of style. Beautifully dressed. Less than ever, could he understand her loyalty to her Hungarian cook 'with her communist sausages, her cabbage and her mash-potato swill. Every one of her meals is an act of sabotage.' Tom longed for Dave, and perhaps also Dave's wife, to talk to.

Tom rang Cora and was relieved to find her in. She so much restored his soul.

Marigold's blue, red and gold actor's caravan was comfortably arranged inside and well-heated against the cooler evenings. In the front was a dressing room and a large mirror in which Marigold, when she wore her blue tunic for the film, looked more like a renaissance painting than that of an early Briton, a painting garlanded with lights (by Ghirlandaio himself?) of a dark, wild-eyed youth. Perhaps through living for a time in the country she had lost her bloated look.

She had decided to stay in Northumberland for the week-end and remain in her caravan rather than in the hotel room which was booked for her. She loved caravans. Not only for this reason the thought had sometimes fleetingly crossed Tom's mind that Marigold might have nomad blood. How that could be he didn't care to hazard since he himself was of no such descent that he knew, and probably neither was Claire. It was a thought best left alone to stew by itself, and although he was a brooder this was far from a subject on which Tom would brood.

The caravan was one of four – one each for the day-use of Tom, Rose, Marigold and Brian (the actor who played Paulus the centurion). It had a dressing room section, a bed-recess, a good arm-chair, a wash-room, an ample corridor with a phone and a fax machine, a small kitchen and a room at the back with a circular bench round a circular table.

At two in the afternoon, punctually, a car drew up. Kevin Woodstock. Marigold was expecting him. 'Bad news,' was what she said. 'The insurance company has demanded that everyone who enters and leaves the studio while it's not in use shall show a pass. There's a double guard day and night, mainly on account of the big crane, I imagine.'

'But you have a pass,' he said.

'I have a pass. But I'm not going to use it to let you in. What kind of a fool do you think I am?'

'Why didn't you let me know?' said Kevin.

'I only found out after you'd left London.'

He looked across the field to the great barn where there were some lights on. 'I suppose,' he said, 'that I could get in unnoticed, but I'm not going to risk it. The police are still on my heels. Good-bye, darling.'

It was indeed a dangerous moment for Kevin Woodstock. Rose and Tom were back on intimate terms and certainly he was jealous. 'Why should he come and take my wife whenever it suits him?' he had said to Marigold, overlooking the fact that Rose had been separated from him for almost two years, that their divorce proceedings were well advanced, and Rose had been in the interim living with Johnny Carr. In fact Kevin needed money. He needed it now as he had needed it when he had shot Dave so neatly. As Marigold had said it was simply 'bad news' that he couldn't just go unnoticed into that studio with her and sabotage the crane.

Marigold watched him swivel his car round and head back for London. Just then a fax came through from Claire. She wanted to talk to Tom with all urgency.

Marigold phoned back. Claire was not at home, only Tom. 'I've had a fax. Ma wants to talk to you urgently.'

'Thanks. She's not at home just now, but I'll wait. What are you doing? Where are you?'

'In my caravan for the week-end.'

'It's up to you, but I think you're crazy. Take care who you open the door to.'

'Don't worry about me.'

Marigold looked at the fax and saw it had come from a number different from Claire's. She faxed back:

'Pa is at home. Marigold.'

Claire, having dinner with a friend, remarked, 'Sometimes Marigold is quite decent to us, quite civilised.'

'Why should she not always be?' said her friend.

'She has taken the trouble to answer my fax. I had her private fax number, you see . . .'

The friend sighed.

Claire got home as soon as she could decently get away from her friend's dinner. She found Tom still up.

'Tom, I had a dream,' she said. 'Very vivid. I wasn't going to mention it, but in the course of the day it seemed I must. It was so very clear. Normally I forget my dreams, but not this one.'

'You sound like my Celt.'

'Perhaps I do. And Caesar's wife had dreams. It's the

crane. I dreamt you went up and fell down thirty feet. Someone had tampered with it. There is a point where it tilts forward you know, and that had been unscrewed.'

'How weird. I've been up with a cameraman already and swung down again without trouble. It's quite exhilarating up there. No director should be without a great crane.'

'I want you to have it examined. Be careful.'

'I will. Where was the crane in your dream?'

'In a huge studio barn in Northumberland. Something like yours, in fact. All the crew was there and your crane working electronically.'

'It would take a lot of know-how to sabotage a great crane.'

'I think I could do it,' said Claire. 'It's a question of loosening things, that's all.'

'Well, I'll have it well tested before I use it. I'll be back on the set Monday morning. It's so beautiful in Northumberland.'

'Marigold is there to-day,' she said. 'Her fax is working.'

'I'm aware of that. She can't get near the equipment without it being noticed. I inaugurated a pass system on the grounds of insurance. Tell me more of your dream. Any details.'

'Only the details of some people, I think up there in the cage, surreptitiously loosening the limbs and the joints and a pivot. Who they were I don't know. But they meant you harm.'

'It's so very difficult,' said Tom, 'to realise that one makes enemies, especially in one's family. It's not real.'

CHAPTER SIXTEEN

'What we are doing,' Tom told his crew, 'is real and not real. We are living in a world where dreams are reality and reality is dreams. In our world everything starts from a dream.'

He had phoned Claire. 'There's nothing wrong with the crane, It's lovely. We're busy now, up to the neck.'

A vaguely familiar dark Volkswagen came up the drive. Claire, looking out from an annex to the kitchen where she had been sorting out the flowers, had a slight sensation of tiresomeness which she soon located. It was Jeanne. 'Oh God!' thought Claire. 'To what do I owe this visit, what's wrong with her now?'

What was wrong was that her role as Marie-Antoinette being amply fulfilled Jeanne had been laid off. She made this known to Claire without so much as a good-morning. Claire knew by now that Jeanne was by nature incapable of considering anybody else's problems. If she could have got into 10 Downing Street with her gripe she would have felt herself entitled to total attention.

Why had Tom picked her in the first place? Claire thought back, how Tom, after his fall, in a state of confusion had hankered after the original girl. He felt that even the actress who had played her part, Jeanne, was his true hamburger girl, his obsession. He had even dreamed of changing his will in her favour, oblivious to the fact that she was only playing a part in his film. But how, why, had he picked on this thoroughly objectionable nuisance?

'I can't speak for Tom,' Claire said. 'But I have a very busy day ahead of me.' She went on cutting the stems of her flowers ready to put them in vases. Jeanne helped herself to a chair and sat down.

'Tom can't get rid of me so easy,' said the girl. It seemed to Claire that Jeanne was going to faint. Her face was grey-white; she was shaking.

'You look ill,' said Claire. 'You should see a doctor.'

'What do you mean by that?' said Jeanne.

'What have you been taking? What pills?'

'What do you mean?'

'You look bad. Why don't you let me arrange for you to see a doctor?'

'I'll see my lawyer.'

'Perhaps you'd better do that. Is Marigold paying your lawyer's bill?'

'No, she isn't. You only think of money. Why should Marigold pay for me?'

Claire simply didn't believe her. She got rid of Jeanne eventually by promising to 'talk to Tom.' Later, Claire was glad that she had called after Jeanne, kindly: 'Try to get some sleep. You need some rest.'

Jeanne found Marigold absent from her caravan and from the set when she got there next day. Tom, working in the open, noticed her and vaguely wondered what she was doing there. She seemed pleased with herself. Hadn't she been paid off?

Tom had a lot on his mind, he and the main members of his crew were out shooting in his built-up fortified Roman town, but a good deal of activity was going on in the great shed. The crane had been brought there and lowered. Jeanne walked to the crane so decisively and jauntily that no one felt obliged to stop her. It seemed clear she was on some errand; and so, in a sense, she was.

It had been one of Marigold's bitter confidences, 'I'd like him to go up in the crane and this time come down with a final thump. He doesn't need the crane. These days it is only a director's expensive toy. I'd like to fix it for him, and him with it,' that had worked on Jeanne's drugged brain. She climbed in the open case and worked the lifting gear. On the rising platform, she tilted the pivot-arm to an angle, leaned over it clumsily and slipped nearly twenty feet. It was a very bad thump on to a cement floor. She was killed outright.

Tom looked down at her twisted face as the ambulance screamed to a stop outside the studio.

'Who let her touch the crane?'

[159]

'We couldn't stop her . . . We thought you knew she was here . . .'

'Where is Marigold?'

Someone answered him: 'She's not here this afternoon. She didn't think she'd be wanted. She's gone.'

A technician was looking at the crane. 'Nothing wrong with the machine. She just didn't know how to handle it. What did she want to go up there for, anyway?'

'Perhaps to wreck it,' said Tom. 'Perhaps merely to see what it was like to look down at a crowd of people.'

Later, in London, he said to Claire,

'I'm glad the film is coming to an end. We're just about ready to wrap it up.'

Cora came over, appalled by the disaster. 'Who sent her to Northumberland, Pa? How did she know about the crane? Did Marigold tell her?'

'Oh, I don't know. There was no secret about the crane. I wanted it, I needed it and I got it.'

Marigold had left for the United States. She had given a press television interview at the airport. 'The great crane was quite unnecessary for the film. It was my father's party game.'

Cora was so beautiful it seemed impossible that she could have an ugly suspicion.

Claire poured drinks all round. Both Tom and Cora felt her strength and courage sustaining them, here in the tract of no-man's land between dreams and reality, reality and dreams.